MW00356170

KYRAPRISMA

Tukki Tukki

Book 1

By

Destini and Jamie Nova

Pursuit
Publishing

Published by Pursuit Publishing

infopursuitpub@gmail.com

First published 2016

Copyright © Kyraprisma, 2016
Cover Design and Illustration by Jamie Nova Copyright © 2016
Jamie Nova www.jamienovasky.com

All rights reserved. Without limiting the rights under copyright reserved above, no part of this publication may be reproduced, stored in or introduced into a retrieval system, or transmitted, in any form or by any means (electronic, mechanical, photocopying, recording or otherwise) without the prior written permission of both the copyright owner and the above publisher of this book.
Approval requests can be sent to the following email address:
infopursuitpub@gmail.com

ISBN 9780692761014

Publishers Note:
This is a work of fiction. Names, characters, places and incidents either are the product of the author's imagination or are used fictitiously, and any resemblance to actual persons, living or dead, events, or locales is entirely coincidental. Use of company and product names are for literary affect only and without permission.

Dedicated to our boys

"If ever there is a tomorrow when we're not together...there is something you must always remember. You are braver than you believe, stronger than you seem, and smarter than you think. But the most important thing is, even if we're apart...I'll always be with you."

-Winnie the Pooh-

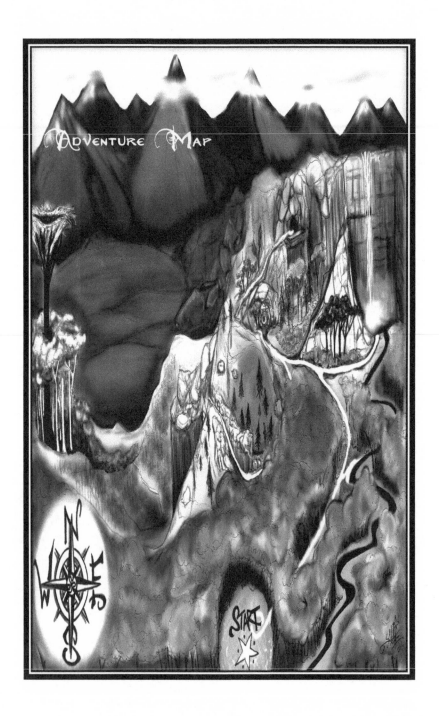

ADVENTURE MAP

START

I am going to tell you a secret that I was forbidden to tell. Most people think of me as a normal human being. I have come to know differently. I was not chosen by fate, but given by bloodline and I inherited a destiny that I could never have imagined. I chose to see what was before me and move forward, and I am glad that I did. It was not easy, but what awaited me, what I was about to learn, I would come to understand as truth. It made me redefine magic.

Magic does exist. I am not talking about magic with cards, or tricks. I am talking about seeing things you never thought existed. I am talking about the kind of magic that usually comes from imagination, pretend, reading a great book or seeing an awesome film. In that world, sometimes our couches become our boats and we are speeding through unknown waters. We make stops, anchor, and get off wherever we want. It's how you visualize things and they seem real to you, at least for a small period of time.

I am here to tell you that other places exist and they are real. Places where creatures that I believed were only a myth became my friends. I have seen some of the most beautiful and amazing worlds that are not realms you can reach by boat, an airplane or a car. I have also seen some of the scariest places, things from your worst nightmares, where your greatest fears exist.

Most of us can't see or get the freedom to see them. I had that opportunity, and I took it. Over the years I have understood it was not a choice, but my path. I have seen so many things that I am not supposed to tell you. But I will. I don't know what will happen to me when I expose these things to you. It is a risk I am willing to take because what I have learned needs to be shared. And we all need to know that what we believe can come true, because it can. Those are the most powerful words you will ever hear.

And when you hear my story, you will know it too.

CHAPTER 1

Trystan and Shane sat in front of the glowing TV screen with their eyes bloodshot and burning. Hours on end, this rainy Saturday afternoon, they sat playing their favorite video game, Minecraft. Trystan ran the controls mostly, as both worked together to create and build a world that came from their imaginations. A parallel universe into which they could escape from the tiny apartment they shared with their mom. Especially on these rainy days, where the walls seemed to get closer and closer, their reality became smaller.

As they played, their dog Koda, who was always by their side, lay sleeping soundly. They did not notice their mom rushing around getting ready for work. She had been talking to them, but neither one was paying attention.

"Trystan and Shane!" Mom spoke loudly. Koda jumped up out of a dead sleep, landed on her feet and barked before she was really even awake. She was their protector and always alerted the boys of any strange noises. The two startled out of their trance with a fright to see a figure standing in the doorway. The light was shining behind it, causing a glow to reflect through its curly hair. Their eyes were surprised as they blinked several times to adjust. It scared them for a moment, but they realized going from their Minecraft world to another reality was sometimes shocking. It was only their mom.

"Yes mom?" Trystan replied.

"Did you hear anything I was saying?" she replied. "I was reminding you guys that it's your birthday tomorrow. Aren't you excited?"

The boys were excited. They shared the same birthday, which was strange for any siblings. Both of them, at one time or another, had wished that they had their own day to celebrate. That they would be more like all of their friends and family, but as the years went by it didn't bother them so much anymore. They had gotten used to sharing their special day and for them any extra day that they received presents, cake, candy, and got a party was just fine.

"Mom, what is MY birthday present?" Shane said slyly, hoping she would give a hint.

"Nice try buddy." Mom smiled and changed the subject. "I can't believe you are actually going to be 8 and 10 already," she looked away in her own thoughts before continuing. "Okay well you know the rules, no video games, TV, or computer when I am at work. So turn it off and do something creative. Play a board game or something."

"Awe.... Come on!" Trystan complained. "Aren't we old enough now to play video games while you're gone?"

"That is not what it's about Trystan. You're never too old to lose your imagination." Trystan listened to her words but he never really understood them. He wasn't one who lingered much on imagination and preferred practicality.

"But Mom we do use our imagination with Minecraft. It's awesome! Trystan just built..."

"Shane, don't talk back to me," she said turning off the TV. "I am not changing my mind. Find something creative to do. I love you guys and I'll see you in a few hours when I am done with work. And please don't eat too much of your Halloween candy from last night." The door closed behind her and the room was silent.

Both boys slumped on the couch with long faces as Koda crawled up into Shane's lap to be pet. Turning to look outside, Trystan saw that it was still raining, so going outside to play soccer at the playground was not an option. Suddenly Shane had a great idea. "Let's play the game with the pillows."

Even though the apartment was small, they had this enormous couch shaped like an "L" which had about fifteen cushions and just as many pillows on it. It took up half of the living room. Ever since they could remember, they loved throwing all the cushions on the floor and jumping into them.

Both boys sprang off the couch and began throwing the pillows and cushions into a big heap. Koda started running around in excitement, biting and dragging some of them from the pile and back to the boys to be thrown again. The boys were jumping from the couch into the pillow mountain, rolling off, and repeating this while Koda ran over and licked their faces or jumped on their stomach. She was a smaller Shiba Inu so she didn't weigh much.

Each time they had to rebuild the mountain, they would change the structure to keep their interest. They really were growing a bit too old for this game, but it was something to do. Once they started to grow bored, they began throwing pillows at one other.

"Pillow Fight!" Shane announced while tossing one directly at Trystan. Blocking it with his left arm, Trystan used his right to throw one very hard in return. Shane dodged it. CRASH!! Over went a picture frame that broke on the floor. Shane simultaneously hurled one back.

While Trystan was busy looking at the broken frame, the pillow hit him dead on his face knocking his glasses off.

"Ow Shane, that hit me in the eye." It felt like dry sandpaper had scrapped his eyeball. "So," Shane said, "I didn't mean to!"

"You never mean to, but you do it and you never say you're sorry. I don't want to play with you anymore." Trystan slid to the floor rubbing his eye, and Shane threw himself on the pillow mountain. Lying flat on his stomach, he crossed his arms and rested his head on them looking out the window at the dreary sky.

Shane was very tall and lean for his age. His mom always told everyone that he was born with muscles and a six-pack stomach. It was true. Shane had big blue eyes and very curly blonde hair. His nose was dusted with light brown freckles that wandered out onto his cheeks. He loved sports, every kind, especially soccer. It just came naturally to him. He was a bit more daring than his older brother and because of that, seemed to find himself in trouble more often than Trystan.

Trystan was a tall kid for almost 10, with broad shoulders and long legs and arms. He wore a size 9 shoe already. His hair was blonde and straight, cut short on the sides, and he wore black-rimmed stylish glasses. He loved computers, video games and to watch YouTube videos on anything computer related. He especially loved funny videos and movies. His passion though was computers and figuring out anything electronically involved. He was extremely quick witted and his mom always said he had the humor of a thirty-year-old. "Quick as a whip," she would always say.

He had always been a smart kid, one of, if not the smartest in his class. He could navigate a computer before he could walk and could read before his third birthday. By the time he was 6, he was already reading at 8th grade level.

"I'm bored." Shane sighed. "Can't we just play Minecraft? Mom will never know."

Trystan looked up at him the way Mom did sometimes to let him know that wasn't an option. It wasn't the right thing to do. He sometimes took the two years older that he was, as having the right to boss him around. When he acted like a parent, Shane didn't like it at all.

"Tryst, come on, what can we do? I'm bored and I just want to play Minecraft."

Trystan was busy in his thoughts thinking of the world they had just built in the video game. They had made this awesome fort with tunnels and lots of doors. Wishing that were his real life, he had an amazing idea.

"Let's build a fort like we did in our video game, but use the pillows, blankets, and chairs too. It would be just like Minecraft, only for real."

Shane looked up with a surprised look, "AWESOME!"

"First we need to clean up so we don't hurt ourselves."

"Noooooo, let's do that later," Shane moaned.

"Shane come on, one of us could get cut by the glass or even Koda." That worried Shane. "And if you help me, it will go faster and then we can play."

Shane put Koda in another room, and then got out the vacuum cleaner while Trystan picked up all the bigger pieces of glass. Normally Shane would not help, and he would have to do all the cleaning himself, but he knew Shane wanted to play and that is why he had helped. Trystan picked up the frame and turning it over, he noticed it contained the photo of his Uncle Kole and his Aunt Greyson. Mom loved that picture and he hoped that she would not be angry. Checking it closely, he felt better when he saw only the glass had broken and not the frame itself.

Shane looked down at a rather large piece that Trystan had missed. Bending down to pick it up, it sliced his finger drawing blood.

"OW!" Shane looked down at the cut and stuck his finger in his mouth, sucking the blood from the wound. Trystan turned to see what had happened. The piece of glass had fallen back to the floor and he went to retrieve it. Picking it up, he saw Shane's blood smeared on its surface. He was about to throw it in the trash with the other broken pieces when it sliced his finger open as well.

"OW!" Trystan looked down as his blood mixed with his brothers. Dropping it to attend to his injury, the glass shard bounced to the side of the room against the wall, hidden from view. Trystan looked around trying to find it but was unsuccessful. He would have to look for it later. Looking down at his finger, it was a small cut, no big deal. He didn't think he needed a Band-Aid, so he did not give it another thought. He was excited to get back to building the fort.

They used the long back of the couch as a wall and put the bigger cushions upright running parallel, draping the blankets over the top to bridge the gap. It was a tunnel. One side was the entrance. On the other end, they used the chairs, blankets, and pillows to create a big tent room. They used a thinner blanket as the passage out. They would have to crawl through the tunnel, to get to the bigger "room", and then could exit out the blanket door. After they had finished they both stood smiling, pleased with what they had created. It did look pretty cool after all.

"Tukki Tukki House." The words came out of Shane's mouth. He looked amazed he had even said anything.

Trystan stared at Shane with a strange expression. Ever since he was very young, Shane had names for things that were not English or any other language anyone had ever heard before. He called a frog a "gack". A fish was "ana". He called his mom "mamaaya". It all was very strange at first, but Trystan and Mom had gotten used to it. They called it 'Shaniese'. They would respond with the correct words, trying to help him learn. At first Shane was very stubborn and convinced his words were the right ones and would try to correct them, even at two or three years old. Eventually over time, they all went away and Shane's special language disappeared altogether.

"Tukki Tukki House, is that... Shaniese?" Trystan looked at him very curious that, after a few years, his strange language would come back again. Shane looked over at him in surprise.

"I swear... I don't know where that came from. I...I just don't know." It was almost as if someone had whispered it to him.

Both boys looked back at what had now been named Tukki Tukki House. "Okay, well, let's go through," Shane said still a little dazed. Trystan just stood there, why did he feel a hesitation? Sometimes he had those feelings for a good reason.

They had no idea what was about to happen to them or the power of the words they just spoke aloud, 'Tukki Tukki'. Nor were they aware that after this very day, their lives would be changed forever.

Chapter 2

Bark, Bark, Bark! Koda reminded the boys she was still shut in the other room while they had cleaned up the glass. Trystan went to let her out as he saw the end of Shane's legs slide into the tunnel of Tukki Tukki House.

Koda ran over and followed Shane inside. It was Trystan's turn to go through. Suddenly a shimmer of light caught his eye. Looking over to the wall he saw the glass that had cut them, covered with their blood, lying on the floor. The rain had stopped and a bright beam of sunlight shone through the window, illuminating the piece of glass. It projected a reflection on the wall that caught Trystan's eye. It looked like a big ball of glass shards. *Well that is interesting*, Trystan thought to himself. The projection was very bright and had an otherworldly glow.

He did not know that the night of Halloween and the following day, it was believed that the veil between worlds was the thinnest. The in-between. The blood of the two brothers had mixed with the light coming through, hitting it just right to create the reflection. This reflection, the Sign of Secrets, activated by powers not visible to the human eye, triggered a portal that was now open. Unknowingly, he was about to enter the in-between.

Trystan turned and peeked into their fort. He could see Shane start to enter the big "room" at the end. He saw Koda go through the blanket door and suddenly noticed he could not hear her excited barks any more. Trystan stood up and stared in the mirror at his reflection. Glancing back over his shoulder to the projection of this strange prism of glass on the wall, he felt a very unusual sensation wash over him.

He hesitated before heading into the Tukki Tukki House. Trystan liked to analyze things before making a decision. Right now he did not have any time to think about this feeling he had, or why he felt a hesitation. He had to just go forward.

Bending down he looked into the fort; he couldn't see any sign of Shane or Koda. Getting down on his hands and knees, he entered the tunnel and made his way towards the big room at the end. Shane must have gone through the blanket doorway back out into the Living Room. Trystan felt a slight chill run through his body and he felt a bit anxious. He could not hear them in the living room and strangely, when he called out there was no answer. Normally Koda would have come running back, but there was complete silence.

Trystan pulled back the thin blanket exit door and went through. Everything went dark. It felt like when you go down the stairs, not realizing that you have one more step before you hit the bottom. That complete out of control feeling. Instantly, the darkness disappeared replaced by a blinding light. Slowly, everything started to come into focus. He was standing up, outside, mouth wide open, in disbelief.

Blinking several times, his eyes began to adjust. He could hear Koda running around his feet, her barking finally breaking his disorientation. He looked over and Shane stood beside him very still. Both boys could not believe what they were seeing. They were standing in the middle of a small grassy field entirely surrounded by a deep thick forest. Koda was running in very fast circles around them.

"Wake up," a strange voice said. "WAKE UP TRYSTAN AND SHANE!" It was a female voice, small, yet powerful and strong. Both boys looked at each other and then around them to find where it was coming from.

"I'm down here guys, hello!?" The voice spoke again slightly annoyed. They looked down simultaneously.

There sat Koda right in between them. They looked at each other confused.

"K...Koda?" Shane stuttered. "You talk!?"

"Of course I do!" Koda replied. Stunned, both boys squatted down to get a closer look at her. She looked exactly the same except now she was smiling at them.

"When did you learn how to talk?" Shane asked, still not believing it was real.

"I have always been able to talk; you just couldn't hear me." Koda looked from one to the other. "You should see your faces! You're cracking me up." A giggle escaped her little dog lips.

Trystan squatted beside her, very puzzled. *Was she really talking?* He looked around. *Was this a dream?* He last remembered being in the Tukki Tukki House. Had he fallen asleep somehow? He had to be asleep.

His questions were silenced by a very loud noise. The three of them turned their attention to the part of the forest closest to them, about 10 feet away. They could see some of the trees moving, as something very large made its way through. They could hear very heavy powerful footsteps. Koda took a few steps forward in front of Trystan and Shane to protect them. She knew that those heavy footsteps belonged to something big and her normally upward curled tail fell down between her hind legs. She wasn't sure if they should sit still, or turn and run. If it was something that wanted to hurt them they needed to be ready to run. She sniffed the air. Her sense of smell was incredible. Different scents were like colors to her. Trystan's essence was a bright blue while Shane's was more of neon orange. Her nose working diligently, she detected a strong, bright silvery purple scent. The little pup had never smelled anything like it.

The movement in the bushes got closer and closer to them and they could begin to see a solid white form breaking through the green of the trees. A soft glow began to emanate from behind the branches. Just that quickly, the figure emerged from the edge of the forest as a strong breeze came out of nowhere, sending shivers up their spines. The three of them stood frozen. They could not move.

Chapter 3

Standing before them was a massive unicorn. It wasn't the dainty unicorn you see in books; those were usually feminine and very elegant. This unicorn took your breath away. Pure white and radiating with its own aura, it stood about 15 feet tall from the ground to the tip of its sliver horn. Extremely muscular, it was no doubt very powerful. Its neck, chest, and leg muscles were solid large masses that looked as though they could crush anything in its path.

Slowly, three sets of eyes simultaneously moved from the golden hooves up to the massive head of the unicorn. Its face was distinct and majestic. With nostrils slightly flared, its long golden hair danced in the breeze. Its eyes were the color of midnight, sharp, and full of wisdom. An ice blue lightning bolt poured from each eye like a long teardrop. The creature was stunning. It looked right at the trio with a stern look. They stood there raptured by the life force that was glowing from the exotic beast. Their legs felt heavy and implanted into the ground like trees with deep roots. They could not move or speak. They just stood there waiting ... overwhelmed.

As the mighty creature stood before the two brothers, he knew them with just a glance. The unicorn could see Shane's excitement, fear, and the sparkle of bravery that existed within. He could sense Trystan's mind working to fully understand what was happening to them. It was the older boy's calmness that was most unusual. The unicorn's look softened and the trio's legs did the same regaining movement.

"Welcome Trystan and Shane, brothers of the Tukki Tukki. Welcome, young Koda of the Guardian tribe. Through the magic of the Tukki Tukki, and the power given by the Sign of Secrets, you have come to enter this realm." The voice bellowed with such force that it stopped the breeze and even the grass seemed to bow. "I have been expecting you."

Trystan started to speak but his throat felt like he had swallowed sand, the only thing that came out was a squeak. He swallowed hard and tried again.

"Um...but, but...but how? Why us? How did we get here and what is the Sign of Secrets? Where are we? How do we get home? And Koda, our dog can talk?" The questions formulated in his brain faster than his mouth could spit them out.

The unicorn chuckled, a deep vibrating sound that warmed one's bones. "I will answer your questions in time." Looking down to the little pup fondly he added, "Of course she can talk." The massive creature could not hide back a smile. "She was chosen for the two of you. She is just as special." The boys quickly looked down at their feet where Koda sat beaming, chest out and ears forward.

"What is your name?" Shane asked timidly.

"I am Arion. I have been a guide to the Tukki Tukki tribe for generations. You are here because you are the chosen. There is something the two of you share that is rare and very special."

"Trystan doesn't share anything with me!" Shane said in protest.

"You don't share anything with me either Shane!"

"Hey, hey!" Koda barked trying to get their attention. "You do share something! You do!" She became excited and began chasing her curly tail and spinning in quick circles. Stopping suddenly, she yipped, "Your birthday!"

"Our birthday?" Trystan looked confused.

"Yes," Arion responded, "Those who share the same blood, who are born on the same day, of the same month, hold the power to open the Sign of Secrets, the door of Tukki Tukki."

"Cool!" Shane exclaimed, "We have special powers!"

"But why are we here and how do we get home?" Trystan responded with uncertainty.

"The portal to this world was opened because of three reasons. The words 'Tukki Tukki' were spoken aloud. Your blood combined while the veil between worlds was at its thinnest, activating the Sign of Secrets. Last but not least, you both are mentally ready to begin your journey. The Sign of the Secrets appears differently to everyone. The only way for you to return home is by passing a series of tests and gathering the rewards. By accomplishing these, the doorway between this world and yours shall be reopened."

"Tests? I hate tests!" Shane pouted.

"I don't think these are going to be the kind of tests that we have at school Shane." Trystan looked up at Arion, "Right?"

"You are wise Trystan. It will be your critical way of thinking, as well as your focus, that you will need to be successful on your journey. You are unique and it will be these talents that will be your greatest advantage." The older brother seemed to stand a little taller after hearing these words.

"And you Shane," Arion moved his gaze to the younger brother. "It will be your bravery, athletic skills, intuition, and your determination that you will have to rely on. The rest is up to you. Your choices are something that only you have control over. Your job is to learn to master every step you take."

He turned to address both of them, "You must learn to work together, to see the other's strengths as well as weaknesses. Learn to rely on and trust each other. You are brothers and there is nothing greater than the bond you share."

While Arion was talking to the boys, Koda had become quite distracted by a very large frolicking grasshopper. A hunter by nature, she had begun to stalk her newfound prey. Pouncing, she landed short, missing by just a few inches. The big bug leapt and Koda bounded after it. It had become a very fun game as she, mimicking the insect's actions, hopped around the tall grasses of the valley. Hop, pounce, hop, pounce!

"Young Koda of the Guardian Tribe," Arion's voice called to her. Startled, all four of Koda's paws left the ground below her as she spun around in mid-air. She landed, eyes wide. Her front legs were out to each side, with her backside and tail up in the air, almost as if she were bowing before the Unicorn.

"As you know," he continued now that he had her attention, "You have been chosen to be the guardian of these brothers. Through the calling of your tribe and the bloodlines of your kin, a great responsibility has been placed upon you. As Trystan and Shane move forward in this quest, it is you who has been selected to protect them. You are to be their ears and eyes. Use your keen sense of smell and trust your instincts. This task I give to you and you alone. Do you understand this?"

The importance of what the Unicorn was saying to Koda caused her spirit to be calm, her gaze to sharpen and ears to stand alert. The pup whose playful energy just moments ago had her chasing the grasshopper, was now paying full attention and seemed a bit humbled and respectful to these powerful words.

She responded, "Yes Great One, I, Koda of the Guardian Tribe, understand these tasks that have been given to me by fate and by the calling of my kin. I will do my best and will guard them with my life." Saying this she bowed deeply before Arion. He lowered his horn and gently touched the top of her head with its tip. There seemed to be a shimmer of light around the young pup as this happened and afterwards she stood with her shoulders back and head raised a bit higher than before.

A sudden shade fell over the field interrupting their discussion. As the unicorn stood still in calm, the other three looked up at what was blocking the sun. It was then that they saw what hovered in the sky.

CHAPTER 4

The ominous shape moved above them, as a chill ran through the valley. The feeling of death was heavy upon them. Arion did not move or show any sign of worry. He already knew what glided above and the danger it threatened.

The boys stood still. Their energy was fixated on the huge beast that stole their sun. It was an enormous black owl with the wingspan of a very large boat and whose eyes glowed a deep yellow. Searching...searching, it could smell their young human flesh and it made the beast very hungry.

"I think we should run," whispered Koda. Arion spoke calmly, "Do not run. Walk with me. Never run from anything that is hunting you. That will only feed its power and it will target you to be its next prey. Follow me."

They walked slowly within the protective shield of the unicorn's magic and were soon immersed into the sheltering arms of the thick forest. Just inside, they turned to peer out from under the canopy of leaves and saw the great owl searching for the meal it thought it had smelled. They watched relieved as it circled a few more times and flew away.

The boys realized that they were about to begin a very dangerous journey. Koda stood instinctually beside them with the very same thought. She began to mentally prepare for her new role and knew it would be key to the fate of her boys.

In the safety of the forest, Arion began to speak. "Now it is time for you to begin. Koda come." She walked and sat astute at the golden hooves. "Do you see those two large sister trees with their branches connected?" Koda turned and immediately saw what the Unicorn spoke of. "Just beneath their roots, you will find a pack. Bring it to them."

With purpose, she ran to follow through with the command. At once she saw it hidden under the intertwined roots. She inched between them on her belly and grabbed on to one of the shoulder straps with her teeth, dragging it out from the dark hiding place. With pride, she quickly brought the pack and placed it in front of the boys.

It was a seemingly normal backpack, brown in color, made of a heavy canvas with three leather pull ties that tightened to close the top. Trystan bent down and opened it up carefully. Inside he could see there were several small metallic stone-like objects and a few other things, but his attention was drawn to a curious wooden box that had a strange symbol engraved into its top. He was immediately drawn to it. Removing it from the bag he stood up and looked at Shane and Arion.

"What you see is the rune of the Tukki Tukki. The mark of your tribe." Arion's voice was calm and strong.

"Open it Trystan," Shane said in anticipation. Trystan carefully examined the object on all sides. After analyzing each angle his eyes found a small latch on the bottom of the box. He opened it very slowly.

At once the box came alive. The sounds of small gears churning inside began to expose what it held. Slowly opening like a flower to the morning sun, the box revealed a beautiful crystal inside. It looked like hundreds of small crystal pieces in different formations, fit together to create an imperfect globe about the size of a baseball. It reminded Trystan of the reflection he had seen, the Sign of Secrets, the portal. The boys were captivated, by not only its beauty, but by its pulse. It was alive, and they could feel it. Trystan looked over at the Unicorn with question in his eyes. Arion smiled.

"What you hold is something of great power. It is the Prism of the Tukki Tukki. Your responsibility is to learn how to use it and to protect it from those who will want steal it. Now, place it in your palm and open it."

Shane observed as Trystan picked it up and was surprised by the weight of it. It was heavier than it looked. He opened his palm waiting for it to do something. But nothing happened. The confused two looked at the Unicorn once again with need for more direction.

"Well that was exciting," Trystan said sarcastically. Arion shook his head patiently. "You need to learn to open it."

Shane grabbed it and started to inspect it. It reminded him of the geodes he had found and broke open with his uncle. Geodes looked like a normal rock on the outside, but when you broke them open there was a beautiful formation of crystals on the inside. The Prism reminded him of those except turned inside out. The light reflected beautifully off of all its harsh edges.

"How do we open it?" Shane replied impatiently. The unicorn responded, "With your mind, focus on the prism and will it to open." Shane immediately squinted in concentration but again nothing happened. Trystan wanted to try again. He asked for the prism back from Shane who placed it in his palm. Taking a few steps back, he quieted his mind. All of his focus went towards the prism. Suddenly he felt a beam of white light connecting him to the prism, and it to him. He centered his concentration on it.

Within seconds, a transparent milky bubble separated them from the outside world and surrounded them entirely. It was thin enough that they could still make out the foliage, branches, and plant life of the forest. Yet, what they saw outside of the prism's sphere was somewhat blurry, as if they were looking at their surroundings through a cloudy glass. Trystan, Shane, and Koda stood there inside the prism's bubble, eyes wide, confused and amazed by what they were observing.

Arion's deep voice filled their ears. "The prism that you hold in your hand contains a mighty magic. The elders of this land found a way to harness their great magic within this sacred prism. It is my honor to pass it down to you now. This prism will provide you with considerable knowledge, direction, and understanding of the world that will be revealed to you. It also holds the key to your path back to your world, the place that you call home." Arion took a few mighty steps closer to the three of them and continued.

"Trystan, you have an understanding of this prism beyond what you have even begun to realize. With your focus and concentration, you have opened the interface and are beginning to find your powers. Now, with that same clarity speak of what you seek. Let's start with something fairly simple, like finding where you are."

Trystan was still a bit overwhelmed and confused. His brain felt muddy and he hated that feeling. He knew he was smarter than most kids his age and when he couldn't figure something out it frustrated him.

"Well, er...." He stammered, "I...uh, I don't know what to do. What do you mean?"

"Trystan, what about a map? Remember in the woods back home Mom showed us how to use a map to find where we are on the GPS?" Shane's face was beaming. Sometimes his older brother just thought too much and missed the simple things that were right in front of his face.

Trystan smiled at his younger brother and in a joking matter slapped the palm of his free hand to his forehead, "Of Course!"

"MAP," Trystan spoke, they all waited to see what was going to happen. Suddenly, the cloudy surface seemed to shift and at once a large map projected onto the sphere's transparent inner wall. It was very detailed and gave them a birds-eye view of the ground.

"This is only one of the many uses of this prism. Let us continue. To close this projection, simply say, "CLOSE

MAP." Trystan obeyed and the map disappeared in an instant.

"Within the prism there are writings taken from the journals of the Tukki Tukki. You are not the first of your tribe to cross through into this world and you may not be the last." The three stood listening to the Unicorn's instructions, transfixed in disbelief, hanging onto every word, and a little scared.

"There have been messages left to you within the prism. It will be your responsibility to find and understand them to reveal your way in this world and return back to your own. They can be found under INDEX. Go ahead and try it."

Once again Trystan aimed his focus and spoke the word instructed by the mighty Unicorn. "INDEX," his voice commanded with a little more steadiness. His confidence was growing.

As before, the milky sphere changed before them and on the rounded walls of the prism's projection was indeed a large index. There were different titles that seemed to be organized in the form of an outline.

I.   *JOURNAL*

     a)   *Tukki Tukki entries*

Shane, walking closer to the screen, reached out and pointed to *CREATURES: ALLIES: ARION*. As his finger came into contact with the sphere, a life size hologram image of Arion appeared beside them. By the touch of his hand, Shane could turn it in all directions to see every angle of him, almost interacting with the familiar creature. Arion's name appeared beside the hologram as well as a brief written description. Shane looked over to the mighty beast standing next to the projected identical image with his eyes sparkling.

"It's you!" he exclaimed.

The Unicorn chuckled, nodded his head and responded, "Yes child, it is I. You are not the first that I have been destined to help along the way. As you can see, the prism holds a vast amount of information to help you on your journey. Take the time to study it. Protect it for it is priceless. Do not let it fall into the wrong hands for its secrets could be used for evil instead of good."

Trystan swallowed hard. All of this was too much to take in. The responsibility he felt to protect both his brother and Koda was just the beginning. Now there was the importance of the prism, the indefinable future that was unfolding before them, his fear of failing, and the possibility of not ever getting back home. Home. Where he used to often feel bored, now seemed like a cozy blanket to him and he longed to return where life was simple. He was faced with uncertainty. Something he hated. All of these thoughts weighed heavily on his mind and in the furrow of his brow.

With his thoughts no longer focused, the projection disappeared instantly and the prism once again felt heavy in his palm. He carefully placed it inside the engraved wooden box and watched as the box became alive again, wrapping itself around it. He fastened the latch on the bottom and safely placed it into the backpack.

"You understand enough about the prism to move ahead," Arion continued. "You will understand more as you study it. I must leave you now, for there is a matter I must attend to." Arion turned on his mighty golden hooves and began walking into the depths of the woods. Looking back over his left shoulder he added, "Find shelter, this forest is no place for you after the sun leaves the sky."

Before anyone could speak, Arion vanished leaving only a cloudy vapor that melted into the woodland floor. They could however, still hear the sounds of his heavy hooves crushing the bramble below him, growing softer until they finally disappeared.

The three of them realized that they were now completely alone in this strange place.

Chapter 5

With Arion's absence, the forest seemed to become louder. The trio could hear the sounds of strange life surrounding them. Some of the sounds were familiar, the whirring of small insects, a bird's song echoing through the forest, and the bubbling of running water.

These noises reminded them of the camping trips they took as a family every year during their summer break. There were also sounds that they did not recognize, strange squawks and clatters of unfamiliar creatures yet to be seen. A low buzzing sound, as if a large energy source was nearby, hummed a low vibration. They heard many mysterious things that confirmed the fact they were no longer home. There was something about this knowledge that weighed heavily upon them.

A deep sigh escaped Trystan's throat. His mind was racing, trying to make sense of it all, while organizing the information Arion had given them. He looked down and his younger brother's eyes met his. Trystan could see the same questions his own mind was asking. He knew instantly he needed a plan, a direction, to give them focus.

"What do we do now Trystan?" Shane's voice trembled as he looked around.

Shane was doing his best to be brave but his words betrayed him. All of those times that he hated when his big brother told him what to do he now longed for it. He needed someone to make the decisions.

Koda, sensing his worry, gently approached him and rubbed first her face, and then neck and back against Shane's hand. Turning, she gave a few gentle licks to his fingertips and nuzzled against his leg. He looked down at her and their eyes connected. No words needed to be spoken. He smiled and squatted down beside his best friend. Wrapping his arms around her neck, he pulled her close and welcomed the cold puppy nose against his cheek.

"Thank you Koda," Shane said as he smiled fondly at her. Her tail began to wag with pride as she snuck in a few more licks to his face.

"Ha, ha! Stop it, stop it!!" Shane laughed and playfully pushed her away. This quickly became a game, as Koda ran back to him and again tried licking his face, and for a few moments they both forgot all of their fears and worries.

Trystan looked up. The sky hiding behind the great canopy of the forest was beginning to turn radiant shades of orange and pink. The black contrasting outline of the dense leaves against the vibrant sky wasn't like anything he had ever seen. There was a new clarity in his sight. Everything was more intense and he could feel the energy of this place pulsating all around him. He looked over to where Koda and Shane were playing, and through the weight of his reality, smiled.

"Come on you two, it is starting to get dark, there has to be somewhere we can go for the night. I don't know about you but I don't want to stay out here when the light is gone." He reached back into the canvas bag and pulled out the small wooden box. Running his finger over the rune engraved on the cover, it was strangely familiar. Releasing the latch on the bottom he watched, amazed once again of the craftsmanship and design, as it unfolded to reveal its hidden treasure. The prism, now reflecting the shadows of the trees and the burning intensity of the sky, looked even more mystical than before. Focusing his concentration, the prism expanded and they were surrounded in the milky transparent sphere.

"MAP", Trystan spoke with intent and before them a large precise view of the surrounding forest appeared. The detail was so clear. Shane noticed that parts of it were glowing white and moving. He saw the large grassy field where they had first entered into this world, and the edge of the forest where they had fled to safety from the hunting eyes of the great bird. Looking closer, he saw three glowing shapes in that same area.

Stretching out his hand he said, "Look, I think this is where we are!" As his fingers touched the seemingly invisible screen the map zoomed in and clearly revealed three figures glowing white. Two human shapes and one smaller all gathered together.

"It's us! Look! There you are, that's me, and see that little one? That is Koda!"

"Closer," Trystan said, not quite knowing why. The map zoomed in and an outline appeared of the brothers and their little guardian glowing on the map.

"Cool!!" Shane exclaimed dancing around watching the white image move. It reminded him of his XBOX Kinect.

They realized that all of the glowing objects on the map were living creatures. They could see small birds flying overhead, smaller animals running through the underbrush, and a few larger spots that moved more slowly. Trystan knew that they needed to find some sort of shelter. With the threat of these glowing things, it was far too late for them to try and build something.

They all scanned the map, eyes searching for safety from the night. With Trystan's guidance, Shane touched different places on the map, zooming in and out with each contact of his finger. They saw a river to the right of them that seemed to run through the center of the forest. North of it, the heavy woodland began to give way to a mighty mountain range they could not see beyond.

"What is that, there?" Trystan said, pointing to where the trees skirted the mountains.

Shane quickly found the area that his brother was talking about and placed his small pointer finger on the location. Through the prism they could see rock formations jutting from the hillside and what looked to be a series of caves. To the right of those caves was a giant waterfall that fed the river to the valley below.

Trystan continued, "See those caves? I think we should be able to make it to them before it gets dark. What do you two think?" he said as he looked around at night creeping up through the trees.

A shiver ran up Shane's spine as he wrapped his arms tightly around himself trying to keep out the chill. His soccer shorts and jersey weren't keeping him very warm. "Anywhere would be better than here," he added.

Koda came to Shane's side and sat, staring intently at the map for a long moment. The boys realized that she too could see and understand what the prism was showing them. She seemed to be figuring out a way to get where they needed to go.

"Follow me, I know the way!" Koda barked and began heading north. She quickly found the trail and let out a small bark, "This way!" Trusting their small companion and her keen sense of direction, the boys followed her upright curly white tail through the trees and bushes.

The two boys knew they had to move quickly. The light was beginning to fade as Arion's warning of danger still rang in their ears.

Chapter 6

Koda instinctually found her way to the river. She knew following it would lead them to the caves due north. Because the forest was so thick, she could not see the mountains but the map was engraved in her brain. There appeared to be an overgrown path running parallel to the river. It was almost as if others had come before them choosing this very same direction to take. Confidently, she forged ahead knowing that she now had a very important job. Leading the boys to shelter would protect them, for the time being.

Jaunting through the bush, she looked over her shoulder and saw they were following. She would run ahead, then pause every twenty yards and look back, waiting for them to almost catch up. She saw Shane with an uneasy look in his eye. Behind him Trystan followed, moving the brush out of the way and then wiping his hands on his jeans. Trystan hated to get his hands dirty and moved the bushes away with disgust, but still at a decent pace. The shadow of the night was biting at their heels.

After a half hour, Koda noticed both boys were tired and had begun to slow down. Her legs even felt heavy and she was thirsty. She stopped and sat patiently waiting for them to catch up. After a couple of minutes, the boys arrived, faces red and sweaty. They were exhausted.

"Come on guys, to the river. We need water. Quickly though, we don't have much further to go," she said looking ahead. There was a break in the forest where she could see, about 100 yards away, the tall trees standing protectively with the mountains creeping up just beyond them. In the distance, Koda could hear the pounding of the waterfall. She knew they were getting close.

Koda worked her way down to the river and began lapping heavily to replenish herself. The boys followed quickly and used their hands to bring water to their mouths. It was cold and tasted so good. They had never tasted water that was this refreshing. After the three felt they had quenched their thirst, Trystan began to think ahead. He knew they needed to bring water with them to the caves.

Remembering that he saw a canteen on the side of the backpack, he carefully removed his pack and grabbed it. By the look of it, he knew that it would hold enough water to get them through the night. Filling it quickly, he replaced it on the side of his pack where it attached with a small clasp. He looked up at the sky that was beginning to grow dark and then, BAM! Something hit him in the chest.

"Ow, Shane! Stop it! We don't have time to goof around!"

Shane, with surprise, began to speak and then, BAM! Something hit him on the arm. Instantly, Trystan realized it was not Shane throwing things at him. Where was it coming from? BAM! BAM! BAM! A series of small tree nuts flew through the air, hitting each of them. Koda got a big hit right on her butt and jumped high, while flipping around in defense. They all scanned the surrounding area looking for the source of the attack. Koda could smell a yellow scent floating through the air. Another bombardment came at them, but this time they were all alert enough to dodge the round of nuts as they heard giggling coming from the brush a few yards away.

"Stop it!" Trystan announced annoyed and took a couple steps forward.

Koda stood at his side alert, ready to pounce, her ears moving, listening very carefully. Then they saw something.

Two creatures stepped out from behind the bush. They stood on their hind legs and had the body of a long feline with the bushy tail of a squirrel. Their faces resembled a cat but with bigger eyes. They had two bucked teeth and a mischievous smile, ears pointing upward with a small set of horns on the top of their head.

Arms around each other's shoulders, they were bent over laughing hysterically. Koda immediately darted after them. Their faces instantly turned from laughter to fear. With their eyes bulging as they bent down on four legs, they ran away and up the nearest tree. Koda chased them but they were far too fast. She stood growling at the base of the tree letting them know she meant business. The two small creatures angrily chattered back at her and one of them threw another nut down at Koda while the other snickered. With one final growl she turned and ran back. They had no time for distraction.

"What were those things?" Shane exclaimed.

"I have no idea, nothing I have ever seen before!" Trystan returned.

"Guys we have to go, come on, it's getting dark!" Koda interrupted and ran off down the path towards the mountain. And just that quickly the three were off, leaving the silly creatures behind.

Trystan was deep within his thoughts, wondering what other kind of creatures they would come across. Those two, though annoying, were not a threat to them but the next unexpected encounter may not end so well. He knew they needed to move fast as the evening chill began to hit him.

Finally, they reached the line of trees that shielded the mountain and began to climb. To their right they heard the pounding of a great waterfall and about twenty feet up the trail they saw what looked like the entrance to a cave. As they made their way towards this entrance, they noticed what appeared to be a heavy stone door with an engraved circle in its center. Around the outside edge pictures of suns, moons, and vines were carved into it. The large circle in the center contained a very large rune. It was the symbol of the Tukki Tukki.

"Are all the caves going to be like this?" Shane exclaimed.

Trystan moved forward and examined the large stone door that blocked the entrance. There didn't appear to be any way for them to move it, and looked as though it had been there for a very long time. Vines had begun to grow over the top of it and grass grew all around the bottom.

"I don't know," he whispered as he ran his fingers over the strange symbol and once again felt an odd feeling of familiarity. He pressed on the center of the mark and nothing happened.

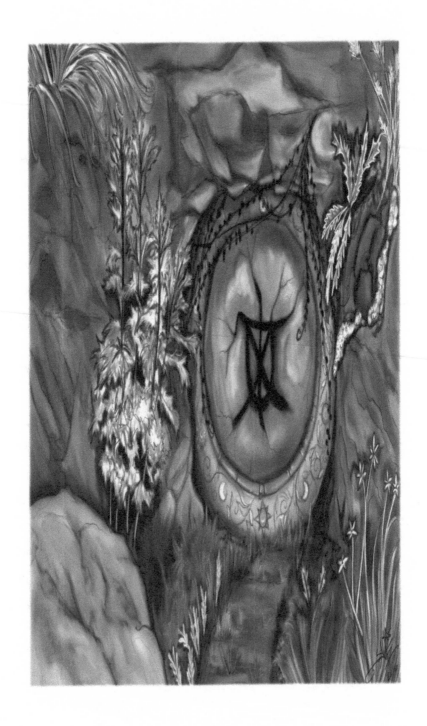

Opening his mouth to say that they should keep moving, he was suddenly interrupted by Koda whispering, "Don't move. Don't talk. Stay very still." Above them in the almost darkened sky they saw a very large shadow. They knew it had to be the enormous owl. Standing as still as statues, they watched as he circled above them, yellow eyes glowing, searching for prey. After a few more passes the large beast moved on.

Trystan let out a breath just in time to notice that he could see Koda moving up to the next cave. It was barely visible in the light of the newly appeared moon. She jumped up on the platform that lay in front of its opening and disappeared. Shane started to follow her but Trystan, reaching out his hand to touch Shane's arm said, "Wait, let her check it out."

After what seemed like forever, they began to grow concerned. Where did she go? Just as Trystan was beginning to worry, her little furry face popped over the edge.

"I found it, up here!" Koda exclaimed as the boys clambered up the path to get to where she was. It was only another twenty feet up but it was getting so dark they could barely see where to place their feet to climb. Moving very slowly, they eventually made it to the platform.

Before them was a very dark cave entrance, about the size of their mom's car. Trystan pulled open the backpack and searched for what he thought he had seen earlier. Indeed, he had remembered correctly. Stepping inside the cave, he turned on the flashlight. The entrance narrowed into a small hallway. He moved the beam of light in a broad sweeping motion so they could see what was in front of them.

"Trystan, I don't know about this." Shane replied.

"Well we don't really have a choice, unless you want to stay out where the owl can find you." Trystan shined the light through the passage but wasn't able to see the end of it. Koda ran ahead and the boys cautiously followed.

"There isn't anyone here, it is safe!" Koda's small voice echoed back proudly.

After about forty feet the cave's corridor opened up into a good sized room. It was bigger than their living room, very cold and smelled of damp earth. The dirt floor was packed down as if hundreds of feet had made it so. Exploring the room with the light, he saw that there were old wooden torches that lined the walls. They seemed to be resting in some sort of metal rings that were fastened to the stone wall. Someone had gone to a lot of trouble to put them there.

"Shane," Trystan called out, "Do you still have your lighter?"

Even though Shane was not supposed to play with fire without adult supervision, he always carried a lighter in his pocket, except when he was at school. He had started doing this ever since he had learned how to build a campfire. Reaching into his pocket, relieved to find it was still there, he walked up to his brother and proudly presented it to him.

"Sometimes I am glad that you don't always do what you're told," Trystan sighed with relief. A mischievous grin appeared on his little brother's face. "At least this time it was helpful."

Reaching up to the wall Trystan removed one of the torches from its ring and handed it to Shane. Running his thumb over the metal wheel the small flint piece created a spark that sprung into a small flame. Both boys watched as Shane touched to the flame to the top of the torch and a warm glow slowly filled the cave as it caught fire. Trystan took the torch from his younger brother and began to light the remaining ones. As the room became illuminated by the firelight they became even more aware of their surroundings.

Trystan was amazed to find how clean the cave actually was. There were no spider webs or any signs of animal presence anywhere. He noticed a large object tucked away in the back corner. A chest made out of wood, craftily constructed with a small metal clasp that secured the top, sat seemingly forgotten. It reminded him of the wooden chest that his uncle had out at the family cabin. Trystan walked forward, Shane closely behind him, Koda at his heels, and found that it was unlocked. Curious to see what was inside, he tried to lift the heavy lid but found that he couldn't do it alone. Shane quickly stepped alongside his brother and helped him try to lift the top of the chest. Successfully the two brothers opened it and were a bit surprised when, within the wooden trunk, they found sticks and leaves, along with an abundance of firewood that had been cut into smaller pieces. It was everything that someone would need to build a fire.

Did someone live here? What if they were mean and dangerous?

There was no other way out than the way they came in. Trystan realized that they had no choice but to settle here for the night and hope that no one would return to find them trespassing.

Chapter 7

Koda knew that, for now, the boys were safe and she made her way towards the mouth of the cave. It was her job to guard them and she took this job very seriously. Tick, tick, tick, tick, her nails told of where the dirt floor gave way to stone and soon she could smell the multitude of scents that surrounded her in this strange place.

Perched just within the mouth of the cave, her little nose picked up the river's crisp dark blue aroma, the green fragrance of the vegetation with the pink scented blooms of its flowers, and the potent rainbow essence of wildlife that lingered everywhere. This was all so new to her and with a deep breath she lay down, ears alert, watching, protecting her boys.

Inside the cave Shane was cold. The sun had set and the cutting temperature of night began to shake his bones making his teeth chatter. He knew exactly what to do.

"I can make a fire Trystan! I learned how last year, remember?"

The younger brother searched the large cavern. In the middle was a circle of medium sized rocks; he knew that this would be the perfect place to build the fire. He gathered the kindling of small branches and leaves. Noticing there were very dry, he set them in the center of the fire pit. He then layered bigger sticks in a square pattern around the leaves. Grabbing a few of the smaller pieces of firewood, he balanced them in a teepee shape with the point above the center of his construction. Taking the lighter from his front pocket, he started lighting the edges of the leaves around the outer edge of the kindling pile. In no time the fire had begun to burn, warming the cave rather quickly.

Trystan watched with pride as his little brother set about this task. He was thankful that Shane had paid attention while they were camping. All Trystan really liked to do was find a long stick and poke it in the fire after it was already built. He felt compelled to say something like "good job" or "thank you" to his little brother, but he didn't. Instead he walked towards the warmth of the fire and plopped down, taking off the backpack, and setting it in front of him.

He felt overwhelmed and scared. This was all just too much. A tear escaped his eye and he quickly wiped it away with the back of his hand before his brother could see. He took a deep breath and opened the canvas bag.

Taking out the wooden box that held the prism, he set it carefully on the ground next to him as well as the flashlight that he still held in his other hand. When he first looked into the pack he had seen a few other things inside besides the wooden box and flashlight, there were small metallic stone like objects. Dumping out the remaining contents onto the dusty ground he noticed that there were quite a few of those metallic stones. Curiously he reached his hand out and picked one up. He examined it very closely and noticed that it too had the Tukki Tukki symbol inscribed on its surface, as did the prisms' box. In fact, all of the stones did. He turned it over in his fingers and felt a small button sticking out. Standing up he took a few steps back from the fire and pressed it.

WHOOSH! With a gush of air and a slight popping sound, the small stone that he had just held in his fingers had transformed into a cot, complete with a thin pad and blanket.

"Whoa! No way!" Trystan exclaimed, "That is so cool, hey check it out Shane!"

Shane stood from where he was just adding more wood to his fire and let out a gasp. "Wow! COOL! I really didn't want to sleep in the dirt! What else is in there?" Koda hearing the surprise in their voices came running in to check on them.

"What is it? Are you ok? What is going on!?" Her hair was raised along her backbone like a Mohawk. This always happened when she was on alert, scared, or angry.

"Check it out Koda! A bed!" Shane said excitedly. She sighed, relieved that they were ok, shook her head slightly and trotted off back to her guard post.

"Really Tryst, what else is in that magic bag?" Shane walked closer to the stones that remained on the floor. He crouched down and picked one up. Trystan showed him where he had found the little button and just like that, WHOOSH! A second cot appeared in the cave. "Yeah! We both have a bed Trystan! Now you don't have to sleep on the floor!" Shane laughed out loud at his own joke.

"Very funny Shane." Trystan was amazed by how relaxed his little brother was.

The two brothers continued to open the small stones and soon the cave was furnished with two cots, there was a slingshot with stone ammo, and a small box. Shane pried open the small container and found it filled with dehydrated meat that reminded him of beef jerky, dried fruit, crackers, and a small round of cheese wrapped in a heavy cloth.

The boys settled into their new surroundings as best they could, called Koda from her guard post, and shared with her the food that they had found. None of them ate very much, they didn't know how long they would be here or if they would find more food so they were very careful to ration it out. After washing it down with the crisp, cool water from the river, they sat on their cots and little Koda went back to guarding the mouth of the cave. Trystan looked over at Shane and saw that he was falling asleep sitting up.

"Why don't you try and get some sleep, who knows what is going to happen tomorrow."

"But I'm not..." Shane's retort was interrupted with a big yawn, "...tired." Within minutes the sound of Shane's heavy breathing echoed off the cave walls.

Trystan's mind was racing with the events of the day and he knew that it would be hours before any sleep found him. Picking up the wooden box containing the prism, he unfastened the latch and sat, amazed once again, as it opened to reveal the powerful treasure within. He knew that it held the secrets that would help them get home so with a deep breath he focused his concentration on the jagged sphere and found himself within the orb. He knew he must search for the answers hidden inside, that the weight of this task was his alone. What if he couldn't find it? What if he failed and they were stuck here, forever?

These were all questions to which he needed to find the answers.

Koda felt very content. Her belly was full and she had a purpose. She had always looked after her boys but this time it held a deeper meaning for her. She was representing the Guardian Tribe, her people. This was her calling and it filled her with a warm sense of pride.

Her eyes scanned the land below and the star filled skies above. She could feel the magic resonating through this place and it excited her as much as it worried her. Even though she was small, she had the courage of a lion. There were moments when she saw herself larger than she was, but in times like this as she defended the cave, she felt very small. The circumstances of the day were a lot for the little pup to take in and it wasn't long before the small guardian's eyes began to grow heavy and she began drifting off into the world of sleep.

What was that? Before she was even fully awake she was standing at full attention, her ears strained seeking the noise that had brought her back from her dreams. She scanned the dark skies above, eyes searching for the source of the disturbance and hoping it wasn't that monstrous beast that hunted them. Not seeing anything in the blackened expanse above she turned her attention to the lands below.

From the height of the platform in front of the cave, she could see where the river fell from the mountains into the forest. The dark outline of their grand branches hovered against the night sky. In the distance, she saw the grassy valley where the trio entered into this land. Everything was bathed in pale blue moonlight. It seemed to dance on the leaves and the moving water. Suddenly there was a flash in her mind, a vision that seemed very familiar. It was a face, one that was very much like her own and that is when she heard it. Not with her ears, it was in her soul.

"Come to me," the voice resonated inside her mind.

Turning back to the cave not wanting to leave her post, she was torn between her duty and the calling of this creature. Fighting an inner struggle, she knew that she must go and seek out this voice. She decided to go but would be quick about it. This decision would change everything she had ever known to be true.

Chapter 8

Bounding from the ledge to the rocky trail below, she was led towards the being that called out to her. Under the brush she located a worn trail and picked up a scent. It was so strong that it seemed to glow a bright red and she followed it with determination.

Wandering down the trail she sensed she was closer, as the voice now became louder inside of her head. It was a voice she would come to know well, one that she would soon depend on. "Come to me," it repeated. And she did.

As she got to the end of the path she saw the moonlight reflecting off the dark waters beneath the waterfall. A mist hung lightly in the air and everything around her was still. She felt calm for only the second time since she had entered this new place. Making her way down to a large rock that jutted out into the waterfalls pool, she felt that it was still warm from the sun. The heated stone felt good to her tired paws as she sighed and stood at the edge.

Looking into the water, she saw her reflection staring back as another reflection appeared standing just next to her. She could feel the glow of the being's energy warm her skin. It felt like home, a new and different kind of home, but definitely home.

She turned to see a beautiful Shiba standing next to her; only it was about three times bigger than she. The large Guardian's eyes stared down at her with great wisdom. She felt the power of this other Shiba, yet she also felt a kindness, like the way Trystan and Shane's mother looked at them. Koda had never known her mother nor had any memory of where she was born. She searched the great Shiba's eyes but waited for her to speak.

"I have been waiting for you to return little one. I am Emiko." Koda's eyes squinted in curiosity. She seemed familiar, like when you meet someone new but you feel like you have always known them.

"Hello Emiko." Koda spoke her name aloud and knew it was not the first time she had spoken it. "Who are you? Why do I feel like I already know you?"

"What is your first memory Koda?"

"You know my name?" Koda was sure she had not told her yet. Emiko nodded slowly and then looked at her deeply in the eyes awaiting her answer.

"Well, I remember Shane picking me up at the soccer field. He was so nice. He pet me and looked around asking all the boys on the field whom I belonged to. He brought me home and then gave me food. His mom came home with Trystan. And then, they gave me a collar and named me Koda. I have been with them ever since."

Koda did not know that the boys and their mom had hung up flyers in their apartment, at the closest grocery and all over the surrounding area. Though Trystan and Shane desperately wanted to keep her, their mom reminded them that she must be someone else's dog. There could be another boy or girl who would be missing her. But after several weeks of no response, their mom finally said they could keep her. For a while the boys were scared that someone would ring their apartment, claim her, and take her away. After about six months they had forgotten about their worries of losing their new best friend. Koda was family and she loved living with the boys.

They were so sweet to her, made her feel loved. She played soccer endlessly with them and would chase the ball and flip it forward with her paws. She hated the long days while they were at school and mom was at work. She waited eagerly for them to return. But the weekends she spent every minute with them. They went for long walks through the forest. She got to ride in the car everywhere they went. They played fetch and she would run behind them as they rode their bikes. She lay on the couch with them while they watched movies and sometimes she got to eat popcorn or peanuts with them. At night she slept in bed with either of them, or she slept on the couch because they both tossed and turned. Sometimes she wanted to just sleep outside of their rooms to protect them. It gave her purpose.

Emiko smiled softly at Koda. Though Koda was speaking aloud, the larger Shiba Inu could also see the images of her memories. Like watching a movie with Koda's voice speaking over it. It was a special connection that the Guardian Tribe shared. The ability to not only hear and speak, but to see what the others of their kind were thinking.

"Before that you have no memory, I see that." Emiko confirmed. "Let me tell you of how you came to me."

Koda's ears perked up as she lay down on the large sunbathing stone, still alert and listening closely to Emiko's every word.

"It was raining hard one night, right here in this forest. Close to this very spot that we sit now, I sat just as I am tonight. I could hear in the distance a pack of Vargen howling. They were on the prowl and clearly had found their next prey. The Vargen are enormous wolves that protect the Shadowlands north of here. They send their young into the south to learn to hunt, train to kill, and act as spies for their elders. They have no conscious and will kill anyone or anything without guilt. Unfortunately, I know them well."

Koda's eyes got big and she stood up as she realized, "So they live...here?"

"Yes, they do. You will learn to be able to sense them. They will come though. Do not worry. They are not here at this moment. The boys are safe and so are you, for now. Rest easy as I continue." Koda lay back down at the feet of Emiko, waiting to hear more.

"We have the gift, the Guardian tribe. We are able to communicate to one another through our minds. You have just experienced that as we were talking to one another without words, when I called you to me."

Koda nodded. She understood and now had an explanation.

"I could see you. As a newborn pup of only a few months old, you could still call to me. You were young so you did not have the power then to call very far, so I knew you were close by. I could see only four Vargen surrounding you. I knew there was probably a few more lingering beyond my vision. I called to the members of the Guardian tribe to meet me just on the outskirts of their taunts and howls."

Koda's eyes grew bigger, "What happened next?" she said completely involved.

"The nearest members of the tribe met me there, these were the Guardians of the Night. They had already seen you surrounded by these horrible wolves and were on their way to you. You see, they have the keenest sense of vision and can hear things, even better than most of the tribe. They are unafraid to go into battle and are willing to sacrifice their lives to protect others. They represent the highest form of bravery." Emiko looked out into the forest remembering briefly the encounter, as Koda could see her visions. It triggered her memory and she too could see exactly where she stood and she began to remember.

"I remember!" Emiko looked back to her and smiled. "Of course you do Koda," she replied. You are learning to hear and see."

"I was crouched at the base of a large tree. They had backed me into it. I was scared, so scared. They said they were going to eat me and that I would be a tasty meal. They were all black and I could mostly see the red of their glowing eyes. It was almost dark. I don't know how I got there though."

"Yes, you were under that great tree. It was a good choice of where to hide only they had already seen you. There were about twenty of us, so we surrounded them and quickly had them out-numbered. The leader of the Guardians of the night, Ryker, stepped forward towards the Vargen. The rest of us continued to narrow our circle in around them. The Vargen that had you cornered were young like you, perhaps a little older, but small in size. They realized that those who were far older, bigger, and more experienced in battle surrounded them. Ryker did not have to speak, he just stared at them and they froze, suddenly searching for an escape. The Guardians of the Night opened up a pathway for them to exit and Ryker pointed his paw. Not a word passed from his lips as the Vargen hung their heads low, tails tucked between their legs, and shuffled out very fast."

"I remember Ryker," Koda replied very excited. "He was very handsome and strong. His markings looked like mine, only he was far bigger. As big as you Emiko."

"Yes Koda," Emiko nodded again with a smile. She was amused by the energy and alertness of Koda. Swift and smart, her brain worked quickly.

"So we saved you from the Vargen that night. It was at that point I was asked to bring you to the world where you would be given your great task from the Guardian tribe. I took you to the land you call home now, to that soccer field to find Trystan and Shane. It was your duty to accompany them here when the time was right. We saw Shane outside playing soccer. I stood beside you and nudged you forward. It was time for you to meet."

"Yes, I remember! I remember that day. I did not want to leave you but you pushed me and told me to go. I had a great task. I can't believe I had forgotten about all of that." Koda paused in thought and then had so many questions. "But, you can go from here to there whenever you want? How? What is your role in the Guardian tribe?"

"That is for another day. One day you will be ready for all of that knowledge. But today, know that I am your mentor. I am here to watch over you. Now it is time for you to return to the boys. Protect them and rest a bit. For you will need it in the next steps of your great journey. "

"But wait, how will I know where you are?" Koda was confused.

"I will always be right here. Not always physically here but I will be here to help protect you. Learn to listen for my voice. I will help you, as you need to make decisions. You will learn to tell the distinction between my voice and that of your own. Now you must go."

Koda stood up, nodded and turned around to find the path back to the cave. She must listen to Emiko and get some sleep. She had no idea what would await them tomorrow. What if the Vargen came back? What about that horrible owl? What else was out there she was unaware of? Before taking her first steps into the trees that lead back to the cave, she gave one last glance back to her new friend. But the wise Guardian was no longer there.

Chapter 9

Trystan had spent the last few hours searching through the prism as his brother slept soundly on the cot across the fire. He had figured out how to move through the prism's basic function in no time. It was very similar to the way his computer worked. There was the basic *INDEX* that listed all of the prism's information. Each of the titles like, *CREATURES, PRISM, JOURNAL*, and so on, were folders that when he used his mind, or Shane touched them, would open revealing their contents.

Trystan logged out of the journal entries and scrolled down to *CREATURES: ALLIES*. Opening *ARION,* he now sat looking at the large hologram of the mighty Unicorn and felt a calmness wash over him. It was like he was there with him in the cave. Trystan read the information that was projected on the wall of the sphere alongside their Guide.

ARION: (pronunciation; Uh-rye-un)

Great Guide to the Tukki Tukki Tribe. Known to offer help and knowledge in time of need. Majestic and wise. A fierce warrior. Son of the Stars.

He felt a little better knowing that they, at the very least, had the Unicorn on their side. He was getting so tired that he just skimmed over the other creatures that were in the *INDEX* under *FOES* and *NEUTRAL.* He didn't know how much longer he could stay awake. What he really needed to know was what they were supposed to do and how they were ever going to make it back home.

His eyes were growing heavy and his brain was feeling overloaded with information. He still hadn't figured out what they were supposed to do. Then he saw something blinking at the very bottom of the prism's *INDEX.*

TASKS: (blink) TASKS: (blink) TASKS:

It was right there, as plain as day. He wondered how he had missed it. Had it been there before? "I must be tired," he muttered to himself. "Well, here goes nothing."

Trystan opened the blinking *TASKS* folder with his mind and what appeared before him made his heart pound in his chest.

Behind a wall of water

Where droplets learn to fly

Lies a passage dark and damp

Unseen to passers by

Beyond the graves of many

Where even more will die

The key to all that waits ahead

Is hidden deep inside.

A dark tunnel? A place where many had died? This is where they needed to go? As he began to feel the exhaustion of the day he closed the prism and placed it back into its wooden box. It was only a matter of minutes before sleep overcame him and as he drifted off he was plagued with nightmares of unknown creatures and frightening caves.

CHAPTER 10

The morning sun shone through the entrance of the cave as Koda's eyes squinted and then slowly began to open. Her fur was warm and she felt incredible. Blinking several times, her eyes began adjusting to the brightness. Looking out over the forest and valley below, she slowly got up and stretched. She had needed that long rest.

Just as she started to take a few steps toward the entrance a large shadow began to move overhead. She quickly stepped back into the shadowed protection of the cave. She knew it was the great owl leaving to make his rounds, searching for prey, almost protecting his surrounding grounds from invaders. She also knew he was not fully aware of their presence yet, which was good for all of them. Once he was alert to the fact they were there, she had the feeling it would be bad. Very bad.

As the shadow moved back in the direction of which they had come yesterday, Koda turned to go check on the boys.

Her paws pattered down the hallway that opened up to the main room. The torches were out as well as the fire. She knew that it meant both boys had probably rested very well. Barely able to see their cots, she made her way over to Shane. Sniffing his eyelids, hair and face, she gave him a big lick on the forehead which made him begin to awaken.

She hopped up onto the cot and lie next to him as he began to pet her soft fur. "Hi Koda bear," Shane whispered sleepily. As he began to wake up, he realized he was not in his own bed. He had forgotten that he had fallen asleep in the cave. The happenings of the previous day began to fill his mind. It was not a nightmare after all. The fire was dead and he was shivering uncontrollably. He looked around in the dark, there was no Mom to wake him up or make him breakfast. There was no soft couch for him to curl up on with his favorite blanket and watch his shows. He had never woken up feeling so alone and scared.

"Trystan…Tryst, are you there? Are you awake?"

Trystan rolled to one side and slowly began to open his eyes. He too had the same experience as Shane. He rubbed his tired eyes, put on his glasses, and as his vision came into focus, noticed they were in the cave.

Yesterday's adventure began rushing back. It was not a dream.

The stillness became very loud in his head. It was cold and he could see his little brother shivering across from him. They were still in this strange place.

"Tryst? We are still here? We are going to be in so much trouble. Mom is probably freaking out by now! We have to go back, and I...I don't want to be here anymore."

Shane's spoke very quickly and with each breath his voice got higher and higher with worry. Trystan had already thought about this as he searched through the prism last night. He sat up on his cot and faced his scared little brother.

"I know Shane, I know! She has probably called everyone looking for us, even the police. I want to go home too, but what can we do? I can't magically open a door for us. Our only way home is to do what Arion told us to do. We have to figure it out. We are going to be ok. I promise."

Walking over to Shane, he sat next to him and looked him in the eye. Knowing he needed to calm him down, he quieted his own thoughts before he spoke again. For the first time in his life, he knew that he needed his brother and that Shane needed him.

"I know this is scary, I won't lie, I am scared too. But we have Koda here with us and we have the prism. I want to go home just as bad as you do. We need to get through this, together. Do you think you can do that? Help me find our way home?"

Hearing that his brother needed him helped Shane relax a little bit. He took a deep breath and continued petting Koda. She looked up at him with her big brown eyes and gently licked his hand.

"I will protect you too. You are very brave. I won't ever leave you." Koda's voice was calm and sweet and it made him feel better.

"Do you think you could build a fire for us Shane?" Trystan knew that if he could get him distracted that he would be back to his adventurous self in no time.

Shane got up and began busying himself with starting a fire. As the flames started licking around the base of the wood, its warmth surrounded him like a cozy blanket and started melting his worries away. In no time, he was back to his usual playful self and was playing fetch with Koda, who had stolen one of the sticks he was going to use as kindling.

Trystan watched as Shane began to calm down and started to relax himself. He knew that he needed to show them what he had learned about the prism. They all needed to have the same understanding about the powers that were starting to reveal themselves inside this extraordinary gem.

"Shane, light a few of the torches so we can see better."

Shane got up and took his lighter from his pocket. Before doing anything else he looked at Trystan, raised an eyebrow into a high arch and said, "What's the magic worrrrrrd?"

Laughing a bit, Trystan replied, "Please?"

"Ok then!" Grabbing the torch, he lit the top and then used it to light the one next to it. A glow began to reveal everything just as it was from the night before.

Trystan was searching for their food. He was hungry and knew the other two must be as well. He rationed out enough food to stave off the hunger pains, and handed some to Shane and Koda.

"This is all we can have right now. We will need to find more food for later, so keep your eyes open today."

"Maybe we should eat one of those squirrely things. They were so annoying!" Koda joked.

"No Koda, we need friends not enemies right now," Trystan said as he picked up the food.

"I was just kidding." Koda noticed Trystan's hand was slightly shaky as he extended it with her portion. He put it down in front of her on the cold cave floor. Before eating it, she walked over and rubbed against his leg to assure him it would be okay. What had he found that made him so nervous?

The three ate quietly focused on their food. Trystan reached out and realized the water canteen had just enough for them to drink now, and that they would need to get more very soon.

Koda broke the silence by announcing; "I saw that great owl this morning flying back towards the direction of the field."

"Strix," Trystan said, as Koda and Shane looked at him in question.

"His name is Strix, and he is very dangerous. I read about him in the prism. Let me show you what I found last night."

Trystan reached for the box and began to open it. Soon the prism's bubble surrounded them. He took them through all that he had learned the night before.

Shane and Koda both sat within the sphere, wide eyed, staring at the information Trystan was showing them. He navigated through the creatures. Starting with *ENEMIES* they learned about Strix and his hunger for young human flesh. He was a gatekeeper, and patrolled the field and forests searching for food, alert for anyone that would dare to enter into his domain. He had a wingspan of 25ft and claws like razorblades. His eyes during the day were like mirrors reflecting the sun, blinding his prey, and at night they glowed a fierce yellow.

"Why don't we see his hologram Trystan?" Shane questioned.

"Well," responded his older brother, "I can only assume it is because he is so huge that he wouldn't fit inside the sphere."

"That makes sense." It was easy for Shane to understand and accept things quickly. He didn't overcomplicate anything in his head like his brother did.

They continued on through NEUTRAL and found out that those squirrel like creatures were actually called Jibbetts. The small animals ate berries and nuts found in the forest. They lived in large groups and once you won even one Jibbett's trust, the entire Drey, or large group of them, would always have your back. They were very silly and loved to laugh and play jokes on each other or anyone who was around. Shane giggled as Koda growled when the hologram of the Jibbett appeared. Encouraged by Shane's laughter Koda tried to pounce on the hologram again and again.

"Ok, ok, come on you two, we are almost done, I am saving the best for last." Trystan closed the CREATURES section, scrolled to the bottom of the *INDEX* where he found *TASKS*, and opened it.

"Listen carefully guys, I need you to help me figure this out." He read the riddle aloud. Koda and Shane stopped messing about and listened.

"Behind a wall of water where droplets learn to fly
Lies a passage dark and damp, unseen to passers by
Beyond the graves of many where even more will die
The key to all that waits ahead, is hidden deep inside."

Koda's head was tilted to one side, her eyes sparkled and she became excited. Now this was an adventure! Shane, on the other hand, looked worried. The thought of graves and dead things did not seem fun at all, but he knew that he wanted to get back home to his bed, his Xbox, and his mom even more than he was afraid so, he read the passage again and had an idea.

"Where droplets learn to fly...well that would mean that water is in the air right?"

"That is what I was thinking," Trystan responded, "Go on."

"Well, there are only a few times I can think of that water is in the air; when it rains, when waves crash against the rocks and water sprays everywhere, and waterfalls. There is a waterfall really close by. Do you think it may have something to do with that?"

"Of course! The waterfall! How did I miss it?"

"Sometimes you miss things that are right in front of your face," Shane said jokingly, kind of. He flinched expecting his big brother to punch him in the arm for saying something like that and was surprised when Trystan agreed with him instead.

"You're right Shane, I do. The tasks were there the whole time and I didn't see it until last night when I had nearly given up. I sure am glad I have you around." Shane was surprised by the comment but loved to see pride in his brother's eyes as Trystan smiled at him. His brother continued, "So if the riddle is talking about the waterfall the second line says that there should be some sort of cave or tunnel behind it. We should go and check it out!"

"Follow me!" Koda jumped up to lead them out of their cave. She stopped just short of the entrance and searched the sky for Strix but he was not around. "Keep your eyes out for him! We all need to keep watch!" She continued off the platform at the mouth of the cave and down to the trail below.

Trystan grabbed the backpack, placed the prism and flashlight inside, and attached the canteen. The brothers followed their little pup, filled with a new excitement. They were on a real adventure, something like they had read about in their books, played on their video games, but never experienced in real life.

Seeing Koda's white curly tail disappearing down the path, Trystan and Shane both moved a little faster. Shane was very athletic and loved this challenge. He jumped from rock to rock, balancing on the exposed roots of the trees that crossed in front of him, and gracefully made his way down the mountain.

Trystan was a bit clumsier than his younger brother and wasn't as nimble, nor could he follow as quickly. He made his way between the large rocks and tripped over the roots in the pathway. His feet had seemed to find the only loose gravel on the trail. Losing his footing, he began to slide, gravity pulling him down the mountainside. Putting his hand out behind him to catch his fall, he succeeded in stopping himself while acquiring some nice deep scrapes across his palm.

"Ouch," he growled, low enough so Shane wouldn't hear and wiped his hands on his jeans. He was bleeding a little bit and he also could see that there were some small pebbles in the cuts. He sat there for a moment and picked the rocks out of his wound. Not wanting the other two to know that he had hurt himself, he quickly stood back up and continued down in the direction that Shane and Koda had gone.

Finally making his way down the trail that wound around the entrance to the sealed cave, he caught up. Shane and Koda were sitting there waiting for him and staring at the large round stone door that sealed the entrance. There was something about it that pulled at Trystan as well, deep inside him, and he joined his brother and little pup. The three of them sat staring only a minute before Koda licking the wound on his hand snapped Trystan out of his trance like state. He winced with the pain of it but didn't make a noise. He didn't want his brother to know he had fallen. Koda was gentle and had cleansed it quickly. She said nothing but looked at him lovingly, assuring him she would not tell his secret.

"I can hear the waterfall over this way," Koda said, "We should keep going." She trotted off down the trail and again the boys followed their little guardian. They came to a place where the path split. The trail to the right headed down to the large sunbathing stone that overlooked where the water gathered at the base of the waterfall. The trail to the left seemed to head directly to the waterfall itself, closer to the stone cliffs where the water cascaded down.

"Which way do you want to go?" Koda looked back at her boys waiting for their decision. Shane didn't have any idea so he too looked to his big brother.

"Let me look at the map," Trystan said as he pulled the prism from his pack. He opened it with his mind and quickly accessed the map. With Shane's help he located the trail that they were on and the waterfall that was ahead of them. Shane touched the area surrounding the waterfall and zoomed in on it. There on the sphere's wall was what looked like a live video feed of the waterfall. They could see the water cascading down the mountain to where it went into a free fall to the pool below.

"Closer," Trystan spoke clearly and it zoomed in even further, displaying a clear image of the sheer rock face of the cliff with a small trail that seemed to hang along its edge with the water rushing down. Trystan squinted and thought he saw something. "What is that...right there?" He pointed directly to the center of the waterfall and with his thoughts the image was enlarged again. Hidden behind the falling water, there was a dark opening in the rock.

"We found it!" Shane's voice was filled with excitement. "That must be the cave the riddle was talking about!"

Trystan took a deep breath and nodded his head. He knew that it was where they were supposed to go. That was where the prism was guiding them.

Little did they know what creatures awaited them in that cave, the dangers that lurked in the darkness, and the secrets that were hidden in its depths.

CHAPTER 11

As Trystan started to put the prism away, Shane had found a bush filled with large red berries. He was so hungry and the plump fruits looked delicious. He was about to pop one into his mouth when Koda grabbed his shirtsleeve, making him miss. The berry hit his cheek, leaving a juicy red mark.

"Koda! Why did you do that?" Shane questioned, somewhat frustrated, his stomach growling. He used his shirtsleeve to wipe off his cheek.

"What if they aren't safe, or even poisonous? You could get very sick and die!" Koda licked his hand, "I couldn't live with myself."

Trystan re-opened the prism and went to the plant and mineral identification. He walked toward the bush and focused his mind on the berries. Within seconds the prism identified the bush and berries and the information was projected onto its wall.

ASZURE BUSH:

A medium sized shrub with small leaves that are light green in color. Located in mountainous regions. Easily identified by its dark red berries. Deceptively sweet smelling, they are large in size and very poisonous. Can lead to death if eaten.

Shane sat there very still for a second, realizing the consequences of his actions in this world were not the same as at home. "Koda Bear. You saved me." Shane reached down and scooped his pup into his arms, nuzzling his face into her soft coat. "You really are the best little guardian ever." He set her down and gave her a few extra scratches behind her ears and along her back.

"It is my duty. You and Trystan are my life." She smiled at him feeling proud.

"Well it wasn't a bad idea Shane," Trystan encouraged, "We do need to look for food, let's see if the prism can show us any plants or berries that we can eat, but we need to hurry. We need to get to that cave."

Consulting the prism, they found that there were two different plants in the area that produced fruit safe to eat. One bush had large yellow star shaped berries called Sunberries. The other was the Aldervine that grew along the forest floor producing large, purple tomato looking fruit.

All three of them took a moment to study what the plants and berries looked like so they could keep an eye out for them.

As Trystan put the prism away he grabbed a piece of the dried meat he had been saving from his breakfast and handed it to Shane. He knew his little brother was getting hungry and he had a feeling that he would need him to be focused and strong for whatever waited for them in that cave. Shane was surprised. It wasn't normal for Trystan to share things with him.

"But, aren't you hungry Tryst?"

"I am, but I will be ok." Trystan shrugged and then slung the backpack over his shoulder. "Come on, let's get going." He scanned the skies for Strix but there was no sign of the gigantic owl. They were safe, for now.

As Shane munched on the jerky strip, the three headed up the path to the left. The path started growing steeper and more dangerous as they neared the waterfall. The forest ground started to give way to small stones and debris that had fallen off the sheer, stone, walls of the cliffs. They noticed that there was a light mist hanging in the air, and with the sun shining brightly above they were surrounded by a mighty rainbow. The spray from the falling water soaked the plants and stones along the path making it slick beneath their feet.

"Be careful guys," Koda warned, looking back over her shoulder. "It is starting to get really narrow and very slippery."

Trystan and Shane looked ahead and saw that the trail continued along the rock wall. To the left was the enormous stone bluff and to the right, empty space. The water plummeted at least 50ft straight down crashing into the lagoon below. The roar of the waterfall grew louder as they approached and soon they could barely hear each other speak. Before heading out to where the trail became a thin ledge, Trystan, Koda, and Shane regrouped. They quickly decided that Koda should go and check it out first to make sure that there was nothing dangerous waiting to attack them. Shane would go next and then Trystan.

Koda headed down the narrow trail and the boys could see her almost leaning into the cliff as she made her way towards the mighty waterfall. They watched her go as far as they could before she was enveloped in a cloud of mist and spray. Shane felt a heavy feeling in his stomach as they waited for a signal from Koda. He hated being separated from her and realized that he would do anything to protect her from danger as well.

"What is taking so long Trystan? She should be back by now! That's it, I am going after her!" Shane started to go down the trail but Trystan caught hold of his arm.

"Be patient Shane and trust Koda, just wait a few more minutes. If she isn't back by then we will both go, together, and see what is happening. Ok?"

"Ok, but I don't like it."

They waited only a few seconds before a very wet little Shiba face appeared from the mist.

"It's safe! Follow me and watch your step! It is very slippery!" Koda barked and headed back.

Shane went first, placing one foot in front of the other and taking his time. He knew he had to be careful. Slippery surfaces could be tricky, he remembered trying to cross a river once over a fallen tree trunk. Unfortunately for him it didn't go so well. He was showing off and not taking his time when he lost his footing on the water soaked wood and fell right into the freezing cold water breaking his toe. He wasn't able to play soccer for three weeks. Shuddering at the memory, he continued moving very slowly along the ledge.

Shane looked down over the edge and watched as the water droplets *learned to fly*. Taking a deep breath as he approached the waterfall, he saw Koda's white tail underneath where the water crashed overhead. Turning and pressing against the rock wall, he put both arms out to his sides and slowly sidestepped until his fingers felt the wall start to curve back into the cave. Continuing along the ledge he made his way behind the water and let out the breath he didn't realize he was holding, as his feet finally stood on solid ground. He walked quickly to where Koda was patiently waiting and squatted down beside her, petting her soaked fur and heaving a deep sigh of relief that he was safe. Sweetly, she licked the water droplets off of his face making him feel better.

Trystan watched as his little brother disappeared into the cloud of mist. He had a lump in his throat and found that it was difficult to swallow. This was NOT his idea of fun. He wasn't afraid of heights. He had jumped off of 25ft tall rocks into the lake where they went camping in the summer. No, heights weren't the problem. The problem was how clumsy he was. What if he tripped or slipped and fell off the cliff? How would they ever make it back home then? He could feel his mind start to race with worry so he closed his eyes, took a deep breath, and thought of Arion. Thinking of the Unicorn brought a peace about him. He took another deep breath. Everything began to slow down and his mind became clear. Shane and Koda were relying on him. Arion was relying on him. He could do it, he would just need to take his time and be careful.

Trystan opened his eyes and looked at the ledge that lay ahead. Only about two feet wide and wet, it scared him. He took a few more deep breaths, in and out, in and out.

Shaking off his fear, he began heading towards the hidden cave behind the waterfall. He knew that Shane and Koda were waiting for him. Hugging the rock face, his arms outstretched to either side, he very slowly started to shimmy his way along the ledge.

"Just don't look down," he told himself, "Don't look down."

It was only about twenty feet from the where the trail stopped and the ledge went behind the waterfall, but as Trystan looked ahead it seemed to stretch for miles. One small step and then another he continued along the slippery path, looking forward and not down. Down to where the water pounded into the rocks and pool below. He glanced back the way he had come and noticed that he had made it halfway.

Breathing a little sigh of relief, he looked back to his destination and cautiously continued forward. Sliding his front foot forward and then his back foot, inching along like a caterpillar, he was almost there. Roaring of the water pounded in his ears, it was deafening. He could feel the cold spray against his face, soaking his hair and his clothes. He watched the water as it cascaded down. Very far down. He followed the water trail all the way, realizing even more how high up he was. Frozen with terror he stopped. He had looked down. Clinging to the cliff he couldn't move, he couldn't think. Fear overcame him and he cried out for help.

"Help me!" He barely squeaked out. "Help me!" His voice became a little louder. The rushing water was so loud he wondered if they could even hear his cries. His fingers were white as they gripped the drenched rocks, feeling like he was losing his grip he cried out again, "HELP!!!"

The sound of the pounding water echoed loudly within the cave entrance as Shane and Koda waited for Trystan to join them. He should be here by now; it wasn't that far to go. Koda started to worry and then she heard something. She wasn't quite sure what it was so she perked her ears and strained, listening with all her might. Through the crashing of water, it came to her, a distant cry for help and the flash of a vision. Trystan was frozen in fear on the cliff wall.

"It's Trystan! Shane I think he is in trouble! We need to help!" Koda's voice trembled with worry. She began making her way out along the slippery ledge when Shane stopped her. He patted the small guardian on the head and in a very brave voice said, "I've got this."

Shane made his way out onto the wet path and pressed himself against the cliff face. Carefully he made his way back around the corner and as he looked ahead could see his older brother paralyzed with fear and gripping the rocks for dear life. Trystan's eyes were squeezed tightly shut while his lips were mouthing the words "Help me," over and over, but no sound was coming from them. Shane cautiously moved forward and called out to his brother.

"Trystan! Tryst I am here! Can you hear me?" He moved as fast as he dared and finally made it to where his fingertips could reach his brothers cold, white, outstretched hand.

"Tryst it's ok, I'm here, open your eyes and look at me." Shane reached out and touched his brother's hand. Trystan's terrified eyes slowly opened and focused on the face of his younger brother. He couldn't think. He couldn't move.

"You need to keep going, you can do it. I am with you and I will stay right here. We can do it together, ok?" Shane's words began to bring Trystan back, out of his mind and into the present. Trystan looked to his younger brother and his grip loosened. Letting go of the rocks with his right hand he felt his brother's fingertips. Warmth surged through them and seemed to pass into his body, relaxing his frozen muscles. Blinking a few times, he shook his head.

"Shane? Shane... I can't move, I am going to fall."

"No you aren't Tryst, you can do it. One foot and then the other, nice and slow." Shane's encouraging voice helped

Trystan began to move. Very slowly at first, but he was moving. The brothers made their way along the cliff's edge and before Trystan even realized they were both standing on solid ground.

He collapsed to his knees and tried to catch his breath. Koda ran up to him and gently licked his shaky cold hands while Shane squatted down next to him and gave him a big hug.

"I'm sorry," Trystan whispered through short breaths. "I froze out there, I feel like a failure." Ashamed, he hung his head.

"You aren't a failure big brother. It was scary. It was easy for me because I am so much smaller than you. If I were as big as you are it would have been hard for me too. It's ok." Shane placed his hand on Trystan's shoulder. Trystan looked up and into his brother's eyes.

"Thanks Shane, you saved me. I owe you one." Trystan took a deep breath and exhaled the fear that had built up inside. Something was changing between them. Something good.

"Sweet!" Shane replied, "Then you can take out the trash when we get back home!" He laughed as he stood up and dusted off his knees. "Now come on, we have an adventure to go on!"

Trystan stood up and brushed himself off as well. He shook the water from his hair and took another deep breath. He was beginning to feel almost normal again. Taking off the backpack he reached inside and pulled out the flashlight.

As the light illuminated the passageway, he could see the floor of the cave's narrow entrance. It was cluttered with small, yellowed bones.

CHAPTER 12

"BONES!!" Koda shouted. You could see her excitement all the way through her whiskers. Rushing to where they lay scattered, tail wagging, Koda began sniffing around and picked one up. Smiling ear to ear she lay down and began gnawing on it. She knew that they were safe and was going to enjoy this moment.

Shane walked over to where Koda was enjoying her newfound prize and picked one up. He studied it carefully. It was about the size of a chicken bone but thicker. He knew it belonged to some small animal and wondered what might have left them here.

"Trystan? What do you think?" Shane tossed the bone to his brother who had just finished filling the canteen with water from the falling river.

"Something's dinner." He said as he caught the bone. "What makes me worried is what that something is exactly." He threw the canteen to Shane and continued,

"Drink up, I want to fill it again before we head into that cave. Koda make sure you get some too."

Koda stood up, bone in mouth, and made her way over to Shane. She set it down long enough to drink her fill from Shane's cupped hand. Shane took another big gulp from the canteen before handing it back to Trystan. After filling it, Trystan attached the canteen to his pack and retrieved the prism. The box's runes were throbbing with a pale blue light. He had never seen it do that before. Removing the prism from its box he noticed that the prism itself was pulsating, almost blinking.

"Why is it blinking like that?" Shane walked closer, "Is this the first time?"

"As far as I know, I've never seen it flash like this before."

Trystan opened the prism and they were quickly inside the sphere. He was learning how to open it very quickly and it was becoming natural to him. The *INDEX* appeared before them and it was Shane that was the first to notice, "Look! The *MAP* folder is blinking."

"Just like the *TASKS* last night." Trystan said under his breath. Shane watched as his brother accessed the *MAP* with his mind and suddenly the projection appeared, but there was something different this time. Trystan examined it closely. At the top right corner was a number one. Below was a second projection with a number two.

Focusing on the new information an entirely new map appeared with a SWOOSH!

"It's a subterranean map!" Trystan exclaimed. "It shows what is underground! Look, there is the cave entrance. It looks like it leads to a long tunnel going down." He zoomed in on the passage and saw that it leveled out into a long cave deep underground. At the end of that cave was a large cavern with stairs that led back up and out to the surface. This map looked a lot like his video games and he read them very easily.

"I am guessing we have to go down then huh?" Shane looked toward the narrow entrance that led into the stomach of the mountain. "Can you shine that flashlight around and see if there are any torches in here?"

Trystan passed the light over the cave in a giant sweeping motion and stopped at the very back. To the right of the dark passageway was a torch that was fastened to the wall with the same metal ring like they had found in their cave. Shane removed it and with his lighter set it afire. The warm glow lit the area as they gathered their belongings. Trystan put the prism away and they headed in.

"C'mon Koda, it's time to go!" Shane called to the little guardian who sat chewing happily on her bone. Sighing sadly, she dropped it to the floor of the cave and whispered, "I'll be back for you!" Trotting off she followed Trystan and Shane into the cavern.

They headed down. The walls were close around them. If Trystan reached as far as he could to the sides, he could touch them both at the same time. It was the same with the ceiling when he stood on his tiptoes. The cave was damp and the walls had a thin layer of slime coating them, as if a snail had crawled along leaving a long wet trail. The ground was still littered with bones but they were smaller than the ones they had found by the entrance.

Dripping water echoed in their ears along with the sound of small remains being crushed under their feet. Shane was leading the way with his torch, Koda right on his heels, while Trystan brought up the rear. The cave smelled of wet earth and stone. There was also a very strange sickening sweet aroma that hung heavy in the air. As they moved further into the passage, it became more intense. Trystan touched his hand to the slime and then brought it to his nose. That unpleasant sweetness was definitely coming from that strange goo. Shane started noticing more and more slime covering the walls and was just about to say something when he heard Koda give a low growl.

"What do you hear Koda?" Shane whispered. She growled again.

"There is something coming, a lot of something's coming!" The hair on Koda's back from her head to her tail stood on end and her teeth were bared in a snarl. She did not like the feeling she felt or what she could hear.

The depths of the cave began to reveal three large slug-looking creatures moving slowly. Snotty, yellowish green goo oozed from their football sized bodies as they slithered closer. Trystan shone the flashlight on them and when it hit the first creature it let out an awful HISS. Studying it closely he could see their gelatinous mass was reddish purple in color with lime green spots. They had no eyes but had an oversized oval mouth that covered the entire front of its body. As it hissed the large, round mouth opened revealing row after row of razor sharp teeth. The first creature's hiss set off the others and then a horrible sound, like a thousand snakes, filled the cavern. Their awful, gaping mouths seemed to grow larger as they came closer. There were teeth everywhere.

"Gross!" Trystan shouted as he stared in disbelief at these disgusting things coming at them.

"Get your slingshot Trystan!!" Shane called out to his brother. Without thinking he ran towards the creatures, torch up high, and with a mighty yell kicked the first one as hard as he could on its side, avoiding its mouth. The slug-like creature exploded spraying slime everywhere. Shane was surprised it was that easy. He swung the torch at the remaining creatures. Pretending they were baseballs, he connected and SPLAT! SPLAT! One after the other, they burst like over ripened tomatoes and goo exploded all over him. The ooze covered his hair, face, arms, and clothes. He took his free hand and cleared the sickeningly sweet slime from his eyes and off his mouth. Smiling proudly, he thrust his still burning torch into the air and let out a triumphant shout! Koda joined him with her own celebratory howl. As they looked back at Trystan they saw that he had put the flashlight away and had finally gotten his slingshot out, drawing back to fire.

"Too late this time Trystan!" Shane teased. Just as he was about to let out another cheer, the same horrible sound again filled his ears. This time it was much louder. He turned to see the walls, floor, and ceiling of the tunnel completely covered in those football shaped blobs when in unison they let out a deafening HISSSSSSSSSSSS.

"Let's get 'em!" Trystan shouted as he started firing his slingshot at the creatures, they seemed to have gained momentum, attacking a little faster than before. He drew back the round stone ammo and aimed it directly into its razorblade mouth. It was a direct hit and the gooey mass exploded. Koda, teeth bared, was ferociously attacking and pouncing directly on top of them with her nails and teeth, causing them to burst like water balloons. Shane kept using his torch as a baseball bat imagining he was hitting home runs. It was one, big, slimy battlefield.

After ten minutes of non-stop combat, the slime on the floors and walls became very thick and the attacks became more and more infrequent. The trio could feel the building triumph over these disgusting creatures. Just as Trystan nailed what seemed to be the last, moving, toothy glob, the three circled around, eyes darting to all sides searching, but they saw no more movement. Koda's hair began to relax and so did both boys shoulders as they lowered their weapons. They listened for any sound of the terrible invertebrates, but all was quiet.

Shane broke the silence throwing both slime-covered arms in the air, "Tukki Tukki Rocks! We'll beat ANYTHING that attacks us! That's right! What? Keep it coming!"

He began to jump up and down repeating the chant when he lost his footing on the slippery floor and fell backwards into a gigantic mass of gluey goo. His burning torch clattered to the ground and made a hissing sound as the fire sizzled the slime. Arms above him like a prisoner chained to the wall, he slowly began to sink into it. He started to feel the heavy ooze closing in around him.

"Aaagh!" Shane yelled, "Get me out of here!!! HELP!!!"

Trystan immediately reacted knowing that if Shane continued to sink, he would soon be engulfed and swallowed. He would not be able to breath. A sharp HISS, came just inches away from Shane's right arm, startling him. Reacting quickly, Trystan pulled his slingshot up and let the stone ammo go, nailing the creature smack in the middle of its dangerous mouth. Once again they all were slimed.

"Koda quick we have to save him!" Trystan yelled.

By this time Shane could no longer move his head but connected his eyes with his big brother. Trystan recognized the fear well. He knew they had to move fast.

Koda ran over and put Shane's pant-leg in her mouth and began to tug. There was little movement. Trystan grabbed Shane's shirt and pulled hard. The two realized this was not going to be easy. The cavern suddenly echoed the awful HISS of several more creatures. Trystan looked over and saw about five more blobs inching toward Shane, hungry to eat his left hand off. Shane tried to move his imprisoned arm but only succeeded in getting sucked further under the surface of the glob.

"Help me!" Shane screamed, his cry bouncing off the cave walls.

"Koda on the count of three, we have to pull with all of our might. Pull as hard as you can. Ready... one...two..."

Trystan grabbed Shane with both hands, secured his feet to the wet floor as much as he could and braced himself. Koda also tightened her jaws, planted four paws and waited.

"THREE!"

The two pulled with all of their might and Shane began to emerge from the goo. Trystan lost his footing on the slick floor and Shane was pulled even further into the gigantic blob, his face dangerously coming close to being sucked underneath the slime surface. Trystan glanced over and saw the razorblade teeth getting closer and closer to Shane's fingers. He didn't have time to use his slingshot, they would lose Shane inside this mass of...whatever it was...and they might never get him out in time.

"Koda one more time. HARD AS YOU CAN!!! READY... one, two, THREE!"

Just as two of the razor filled mouths opened wide to chomp down on Shane's pinky and thumb, Trystan and Koda pulled as hard as they could. A loud suction popped and echoed in the cave as the air pocket thrusted Shane forward. Launched from his slimy prison, he was hurtled forward and knocked over the other two like a bowling ball into bowling pins. After tumbling down, hands deep in slime they relaxed for a moment. They all looked at each other in disbelief. Shane looked down at his hands, counting his fingers. He had all five. HE HAD ALL FIVE!

The three just stared at one another realizing how close they all just came to losing this battle. Shane knew that he should not ever again celebrate too quickly. It could have very well cost him his life. Their trifecta trance was abruptly broken with the hissing sound again that was moving relentlessly closer to them.

Quick to their feet, Shane picked up his burning torch and they instinctually went into battle mode. He destroyed the few remaining blobs until every last creature was defeated, and then everything grew very still. Looking at the large mountain of slime that had almost swallowed Shane, they could only wonder what it was.

The prism began to pulsate Trystan's backpack and he could feel it awaken. Quickly taking it off, he opened it and pulled out the box noticing that the runes were brightly glowing. They could hear its power buzzing throughout the stone chamber.

"It's green!" Trystan wondered what this meant. "Green...this has to be good...right?"

But what did 'good' mean? They had completed one task and they had two more to go. He logically assumed that each task would grow more difficult, and frankly, this one was already pretty scary. Shane could have died. They all could have.　　What they didn't know was how close they had really come to death.

They had no idea the prism was about to reveal a story of a mighty battle that had ended in a death, in this very spot where they were standing.　A death of someone they had seen images of many times before.

Chapter 13

The three were surrounded by the prism and stood in its inner circle. Its bright light illuminated the torch-lit cave and it was the first time they could all see one another clearly.

"Trystan, I can hardly see you. You look like a big ball of slime with two glass bottles for eyes! Ha, ha, ha, ha!"

Trystan started to get defensive and then he looked down. He did look like one, big, slime blob. He started laughing at himself, and then all three found themselves in a fit of deep belly laughs, partially from the nerves, from the relief that they were all still alive, and the fact that they all did look ridiculous.

"Look Tryst," Shane was giggling as the started to make a curly slime Mohawk on the top of his head. When he thought something was really funny, his giggle was high and very silly. It made everyone else laugh even harder.

"I want a Mohawk too, Shane," Koda begged. Shane bent over laughing so hard he was barely able to lift his spaghetti arms. They flopped back down. He reached up, trying again, and shaped Koda's slime covered fur into a Mohawk. Koda stood on her hind legs and took a few steps back and forth. "I think I have to pee." Koda said in a Muppet-like voice. She looked so ridiculous that they all started laughing even harder. Trystan fell down, laughing so hard he was crying. The other two collapsed on the floor next to him. It felt good for them to release all of the pent up adrenaline.

As their laugher began to fade, Trystan glanced over and saw *FOES* flashing. "Hey look!"

The three got up quickly and focused on the screen. Shane reached out and touched the flashing title but nothing happened. All facing the projection they looked puzzled. Filling up the sphere behind them was a very large hologram of the enormous raspberry colored gooey blob with the biggest mouth and row upon row of the sharpest teeth they had ever seen. They turned around and were startled by its size. Why was it so big? They had only seen ones the size of a football. And then it occurred to Trystan.

"Shane this has to be what you fell into, but it must have been dead already. But, how?" Trystan took one step forward toward the simulated mouth of the creature and touching it the data came up immediately.

GIANT BOOSLAAK: (pronunciation; bows-slock)

An enormous creature composed of a gelatinous slime. Having no eyes or ears, it senses its prey through vibration. Having one large mouth located in the front, its multiple rows of razor sharp teeth are able to cut through bones easily, exuding venom that paralyzes its victim. The great mother, Slamia (pronunciation: Slah-me-uh) is the largest and deadliest of all. One bite from the mother can rip a body in half and release enough poison to instantly kill its prey.

STATUS: ALL DEAD.

Kole and Greyson of Tukki Tukki, Gunner of the Defenders, Trystan and Shane of Tukki Tukki, and Koda of the Guardian Tribe. TASK COMPLETE.

Trystan and Shane stood very still. The names were ones that were familiar. Greyson and Kole were the names of their aunt and uncle. After their dad had passed away, only a few months after Shane was born, Uncle Kole had been the only father figure they had ever really known. Could it be the same Kole? Had he been of the Tukki Tukki tribe as well?

Trystan could not comprehend what he was reading. His uncle was Tukki Tukki? He and their Aunt Greyson must have shared the same birthday if they were Tukki Tukki. Their aunt had disappeared before Trystan had been born and they were warned to never talk about her, especially with Uncle Kole. Mom had said it was too painful for him and it was something that the family never talked about. EVER. Trystan always struggled not to say anything, especially with her pictures all over his uncle's home. He found it awkward to pretend she didn't exist when, in fact, she was everywhere around them.

"Wait, Aunt Greyson, she went missing before we were born. Shane do you think..."

Trystan sat staring at the screen. He noticed there was a link below the description and status. Using his mind, he opened the link. Immediately the prism went to *JOURNAL ENTRIES* and *TUKKI TUKKI TRIBE*. There was an attachment in the log. The name next to it was Kole, but only Kole... what about Greyson?

He had simply written below the video link, "The day half of me died and our journey ended."

"Trystan, open the video.... Trystan!" Shane gave him a light grab of the arm.

Trystan reached out with his mind, the projection went dark then on the spheres wall the video feed began to play.

Both boys grew somber and braced themselves for what they were about to see. As the video began to play, they stood watching in disbelief.

The camera angle showed their aunt and uncle coming into the cave with their German Shepard, Gunner, next to them. Their Uncle Kole looked about eighteen, eight years older than Trystan, and carried a slingshot very similar to the one Trystan now had. Aunt Greyson carried a long Bo-staff marked with the same glowing runes that decorated the prism's box. She looked like she was sixteen or seventeen, the same age as she appeared in the last photos that were taken of her before she had vanished. They watched as the three journeyed down the cave, the exact way that Trystan, Shane and Koda began. Splattering and destroying the smaller Booslaaks all around them, they carried forward on their mission. They had made it through the long tunnel and were just entering the large room at the end when suddenly, out of the darkness on the side closest to their aunt, emerged the great mother Booslaak, Slamia.

Greyson turned and began to attack the large beast with her staff. She was skilled and very quick with her weapon and heard the pain-filled hiss of the great mother every time she struck the great beast. The boys watched as their Uncle Kole began pelting the giant Booslaak with his small stone ammo, trying to help out his sister as best he could while Gunner barked and growled trying to distract the predator.

Greyson took her staff and slammed the end of it into the gooey mass to try and cause even more damage, but something went wrong. Instead of injuring the creature further, Greyson's staff stuck fast in the side. Slamia turned her giant mouth towards Greyson as she struggled to remove her weapon from its slimy prison. The rows and rows of razor blade teeth clenched her arm fast, releasing their deadly poison.

Trystan, Shane, and Koda stood with their eyes locked on the screen as their hearts began to race. They watched in horror as their uncle screamed out for his sister. Tears welled up in their eyes as they saw their aunt's body grow limp as the venom quickly overtook it. The scream of sadness that came from their uncle was one they would never forget. It reminded them of the movie Maleficent, her deep emotional cry echoed in the forest when she lost her wings. They were a part of her, just as Greyson was a part of Kole. His sister, his warrior and partner in Tukki Tukki, was dying before his eyes and there was nothing he could do to save her.

They watched closely as his sadness turned to rage. Slamia was hurt badly by the Bo-staff. As Kole drew his slingshot, he did not use his regular ammo. Instead he pelted her one after the other with the metal stones from his backpack. It was as if he knew with those magic stones, he could destroy any amount of life the murderous beast had left. A final shudder shook the monster's body as death fell upon both the great beast and his sister. Kole fell to his knees, sobs racking his body as Gunner leaned into him, the two of them bridged over the lifeless body of his sister, both weeping mournfully. The video feed went black and the *INDEX* appeared in its place.

Trystan, Shane and Koda stood very still, tears welling up in their eyes. They were incredibly sad for their uncle; the pain he must have felt all of these years but could never tell anyone. Trystan and Shane would sometimes drive each other crazy, but they really could not imagine a world where the other was not in it. Especially now, in Tukki Tukki, everything was changing.

"So that's what happened." Trystan swallowed hard, the lump in his throat making it very difficult. "That is what happened to Aunt Greyson. No wonder Uncle Kole never wanted to talk about it."

Silently, they all wondered if they would make it out of this alive. They knew that if Slamia had been there, their fate could have easily been the same as their aunt's. They realized from here on out, the three of them would have to be alert to their surroundings at all times because all sorts of deadly creatures could emerge from the darkness. This was not a game, not at all. Their attention was broken by a flashing in the *INDEX* of the sphere that was pulsating and distracting their attention from the blob that was previously Slamia. *REWARD.* It blinked on and off. Curious, Shane walked over and touched the highlighted area. Their attention was pulled back to Slamia's giant body as that same pulsating glow from the prism started to appear deep inside the dead mother.

"There is something inside it," Koda whispered, growing very excited and standing alert.

"Well who wants to reach in and get it?" Trystan asked aloud with a grossed out look on his face.

Shane glanced over and saw his brother wincing at the thought. He handed Trystan the torch, grabbed his brother's arm as his anchor, stepped up, and stuck his arm into the slime, right at the source of the light. He felt something long, cold and...

"I've got it!" As he pulled he found that it was stuck deep within the slime. He was up to his armpit in the gooey carcass and did not want to get sucked back into it. "I am going to need your help guys, ready? Grab on and help me pull."

Trystan put the prism away, sat the torch on the floor and wrapped his arms around Shane's waist. Koda grabbed Trystan's shirt securely in her mouth. "Okay, one...two...three!" All three of them pulled with every bit of strength they had left and as the glowing object began to rise closer and closer to the surface. With a final tug and popping sound, the mysterious item was freed from Slamia's body.

Shane stood holding the rune inscribed Bo-staff of his Aunt Greyson. The markings were glowing with the same light as the prism, and he could feel an otherworldly surge go through him. Not knowing why, he thrust the staff high in the air, both hands gripping the weapon high over his head, and from the depths of his soul shouted, "WE ARE TUKKI TUKKI!!" As the final words left his mouth, a bright blue light flooded the cave as a mighty wave blasted from the staff destroying nearly all the slime and remains of the dead Booslaaks.

The light faded and the runes on the Bo-staff dulled. There was a silence that filled the cave, they stood in awe of the power that they had just witnessed and the magic the staff held. With his eyes beginning to adjust back to the fire-lit darkness of the cave, Trystan noticed a second object glowing on the cavern floor where Slamia's giant body had been.

Walking over to it and bending down, his fingertips discovered a large metal key. He picked it up and examined it closer. It also had the markings of the Tukki Tukki tribe. The same ones he had seen on the giant stone that blocked the entrance to the first cave they had found. Turning the key over and over in his hand he was amazed by the craftsmanship and detail in the metal.

Shane walked towards him, staff in hand. Trystan earlier had noticed that his little brother didn't seem so small anymore. He had the look of a young warrior after his battle with the Booslaaks. Now, with the Tukki Tukki Bo-staff, there was no denying it.

Shane bent down and pick up his still burning torch. Wanting to take a look around the cavern, he held it high above him. This room where their mighty battle had occurred now looked empty. The only thing that gave any indication that something awful had happened here was the slime that still covered the three of them and the staff he held in his hand. The Bo-staff of his Aunt Greyson. He, along with the help of Koda, continued to survey the huge cavern. They found a tunnel that lead to a steep staircase heading upward and noticed there was something lying at its base.

He made his way closer and saw that it was another backpack, one nearly identical to the one they carried.

Kneeling, he set down the staff and picked up the pack. Shaking free the dust that covered it, he saw that it was decorated with drawings of the Tukki Tukki runes. His aunt or uncle must have drawn them on years ago. He decided that it would be his now. He had a direct connection with his aunt now that he carried the Bo-staff.

He noticed that there was also a canteen attached to the outside. As he opened it to look inside, he found that it was empty. His memory flashed back to the battle scene between his aunt, uncle, Gunner, and Slamia and remembered that his Uncle Kole had used the metallic stones to put an end to the great beast. Shane placed it on his back, picked up his Bo-Staff, and headed back towards his brother. Trystan was absorbed in using the prism to try and figure out what their next step should be.

"Look what I found Trystan, another backpack. It must have been Aunt Greyson and Uncle Kole's."

His brother nodded only halfway hearing him. He was distracted looking at the map.

"I found it at the bottom of the stairway over there." Shane continued.

Looking up from the map Trystan came back to the present.

"A stairway? Show me! That is the way we need to go to get out of here."

Shane brought him over to the base of the stairs and shined the flashlight up the passageway. "I'll lead the way."

Trystan and Koda followed as the stairway led them up and out the belly of the mountain. Shane guided them with a newfound pride. Torch in one hand and Bo-staff in the other he felt braver than he ever had before. The weapon in his hand felt familiar, like it belonged to him, and he was honored that it was now his to use and protect. Trystan had the prism and now he had the staff.

Their legs began to ache as they climbed higher and higher. The battle had drained them of all energy and now they could feel how tired and sore their muscles were. Through everything they had just fought, and the sadness they experienced as they learned of the fate of Aunt Greyson, there was an unmistakable calm surrounding the three of them as they ascended from the Booslaaks lair. Each of them had changed with the battle, learning their place within the small tribe, appreciating each other's strengths and trusting one another more than they ever had.

They reached the top of the stone staircase and found themselves in a small room. Blocking what looked to be the exit was the large stone etched with Tukki Tukki runes. Trystan stepped towards the door asking Shane to bring his torch closer to the center of the large carving. The firelight illuminated the design. It was an exact duplicate of the outside that they had seen earlier. In the center was what Trystan had been hoping for, a keyhole. Taking the key that bore the similar markings and placing it into the hole he held his breath. The key fit perfectly and he turned it to the right.

He could hear the low grumble of gears awaken from their deep sleep as the room vibrated around them. Trystan took a few steps back. Koda's Mohawk heightened down her spine as she stood next to the boys, prepared for whatever came next. The large circular stone slowly began to move to the right. Small stones, vines, and spider webs fell from the wall. An opening appeared and looked as though it had been carved for the stone to slide over and fit inside.

Bright rays of sunlight began to break through the darkness and shine around the edges of the circular rock as it began to rumble, rolling to the right and fitting snugly within the hidden chamber. They were blinded by the sun's rays and all three took a huge breath as fresh air rushed in from the outside, extinguishing the torch, circling them with a feeling of life and newness.

Their eyes hadn't completely adjusted to the bright sun when their ears were filled with the sound of a deep, powerful voice.

Chapter 14

"How far you've come young ones." The vibrations of the familiar voice moved through their bodies and all three fell to their knees. Arion bowed his mighty head to where they sat crumpled at his powerful golden hooves. One by one, the trio felt the heaviness and exhaustion slip away as he placed his soft snow-white nose upon each of their cheeks.

"You have done so well! You are the first of the Tukki Tukki to have made it this far and you have made your ancestors very proud."

Trystan looked up at Arion, "Aunt Greyson! Uncle Kole, poor uncle Kole! I can't imagine.... I... I didn't know!"

"Yes," the Unicorn continued, "Your aunt and uncle were also members of the Tukki Tukki. They were highly respected within the tribe and the loss of your Aunt Greyson was felt throughout many worlds. Shane, you have many of her qualities and because of your bravery, quickness, and heroic deeds the Bo-staff has chosen you." Shane lifted his head and was magnetically drawn to those large gentle eyes.

"You have started down the path to becoming a Tukki Tukki warrior. This is a great honor and responsibility. Treat it with respect. Do not abuse it. Continue on your journey with pride in everything you do. We believe in you." With every one of Arion's words they felt more rejuvenated, their energy recharging.

"You have all done very well, very well indeed. Trystan, the key that was hidden within Slamia, that opened the Sacred Door, still holds a great deal of importance. You must retrieve it and take it with you on your journey. You never know when it will become useful again."

Trystan stood, feeling stronger and a little less shaky. He walked back into the dampness of the cool cave. There was just enough space for him to reach into the Sacred Door's chamber. He stretched his long, lanky arm in as far as it would go. Finding the key with his fingertips he twisted to the left and easily slid it free. Walking back out into the warming sunshine he took off his backpack and set it on the ground. He removed one of the leather ties, looped the lace through the top of the key and tied it around his neck. Placing it underneath his shirt where the cold metal came to rest on his chest, he softly patted it. It brought him a feeling of comfort and accomplishment.

"Now, go down to the sunbathing rock. Koda knows the way." Arion winked at the little pup and she got the feeling that the unicorn knew about her midnight meeting with Emiko. "You will find I have prepared you something to eat and you can wash up and rest a bit before you continue. The sun has yet to reach its peak so you have plenty of time to regain your strength. You will need it. What lies ahead of you will demand your full focus, attention, and teamwork. What is most important is that you are learning to rely on one another. That is vital for your survival."

"Aren't you coming back with us? I have so many questions about the Tukki Tukki, our aunt and uncle, and..." Trystan's whirring thoughts were interrupted by Arion's deep voice, "No, unfortunately I cannot. I have spent too much time in one place already. I do not want to alert anyone to my presence. I will see you again. Do not be afraid. You will get your answers in time young Trystan."

All three came and stood before the mighty Unicorn. He looked them each in the eye and said, "I am proud of you. Trystan and Shane of the Tukki Tukki, and young Koda of the Guardian Tribe, you have successfully completed the first task. By destroying the remaining Booslaaks, retrieving the staff, and opening the Sacred Stone Door, you have come one step closer to making it back home. Now go, rest, and eat. I will always be watching over you."

The majestic beast turned on his golden hooves and began down the trail, away from the waterfall. He disappeared in the deep darkness of the forest leaving only a mist swirling around the underbrush that was absorbed into the ground below.

"He always seems to do that, doesn't he?" Koda walked to the trail's edge where Arion had left them, "How does he just vanish like that?" The little pup sat in awe of the unicorn as she sniffed the air searching for any remaining trace of his silvery purple scent.

The boys turned to look at the open cave entrance. They understood in depth the great family mystery surrounding their aunt and couldn't wait to talk to their Uncle Kole when they got back home. That was, IF they made it back home.

A loud grumbling noise came from behind the boys. Spinning around simultaneously, weapons drawn, they saw Koda standing and looking up at them, eyes wide.

"It was my stomach!! I am STARVING!!!" A smile snuck across her mouth as she added, "We should head down to the sunbathing rock and eat!!" Nodding their heads, Trystan and Shane agreed that was a fantastic idea.

"Do you know where this sunbathing rock is Koda, or should we look at the map?" Shane questioned. The little pup looked up at the young warrior proudly, "I know where it is, follow me!"

Koda led her boys toward the waterfall and reached the same spot in the trail that ran north and south. The upper trail would lead them back to the entrance of the Booslaaks' cave. They were not surprised when the little pup turned right, down the trail.

The path led them into a beautiful clearing at the base of the waterfall. Spray from the falling water created patches of rainbow all around them and the large sunbathing rock was warm from the morning sun. The water gathered in a deep crystal clear pool that was surrounded by flowers and plant life so vivid the colors seemed to glow. It looked like the postcards they had received from their Uncle Kole when he went to Hawaii. They walked out to the edge of the sunbathing rock and peered into the reflective water. All covered from head to toe in slime and dirt, what a sight they were. It had begun to dry and was getting crusty on their clothes and hair. Even Koda's fur had hardened into a permanent Mohawk.

"Look at us!" Trystan laughed, "We look ridiculous!"

"You look ridiculous Trystan, Koda and I look pretty cool."

Shane tried pretending to be serious but his reflection and those of his brother and Koda made him laugh even harder.

The pup leaned down and lapped the cool water, quenching her thirst. Trystan and Shane removed the canteens from their backpacks and filled them both before drinking them dry. They were just coming to realize how thirsty they were from their mighty battle. After getting their fill of water, the boys washed their hands and faces so they could eat.

"I am starving!" Shane spoke as his tummy agreed with a rumble. "Where do you think Arion put the food?" He scanned the area but didn't see anything. Trystan sat back on his heels and looked around. There was definitely no large picnic set out for them. He stood and walked around taking a closer look.

In the center of the sunbathing rock he found a large metallic stone, much like the ones that they had discovered in their pack. A small button stuck out the side and when Trystan pressed it, SWOOSH, a very large basket appeared. It reminded him of the picnic lunches he and his mom would have on days that Shane was at soccer practice. Those were special days when they had afternoons alone together. He was surprised how much it made him ache for her. He hadn't had time to realize how much he missed his mom until now.

Shane grabbed the picnic basket with a "YES!" which snapped Trystan from his thoughts.

"What is inside?" Shane couldn't wait and he opened it up like he opened his Christmas presents. He found a large blanket that they carefully spread out on the rock. There was a small wheel of cheese, fruits, nuts, more of the dried meat, a fresh chunk of bread, and a handful of carrots.

"Carrots!!! My favorite!" Koda was so excited; they truly were her favorite treat.

Making themselves comfortable, they sat in a circle and began to devour the food. Trystan took a quiet moment to silently thank Arion, knowing somehow the great Unicorn would hear him. As Koda munched on the carrots, Trystan and Shane tore into the bread and cheese. The bread felt warm still, as though it had just come from the oven. The cheese, given how hungry they were, was the best cheese that they had ever tasted.

Trystan picked up one of the fruits and recognized it from his research in the prism. It was a Sunberry, large, yellow, and shaped like a star. Trystan turned it over in his hand to get a better look. He wasn't very adventurous when it came to food. In fact, Trystan would be happy eating

French Fries and chicken nuggets the rest of his life. As he looked at the juicy, ripe fruit, he felt a little change happen within him. He didn't know if it was how hungry he was, but he was actually feeling excited about trying something new. He sank his teeth into the tender flesh of the Sunberry as the juices ran down his chin and over his fingers. His eyes lit up.

"WOW!! This is amazing! It tastes like a pink Starburst!!" He took another bite and then another. Before he realized it he had eaten the entire thing and was reaching for another.

"Well save me one Trystan!" Shane exclaimed as he reached for a Sunberry. Taking a huge bite his eyes got enormous. "This is amazing! It is better than candy even! Well...almost! Try some Koda!" Shane tore a small bit from his piece of fruit and tossed it towards his pup, she caught it easily and chewed it up.

"Pretty good but, could I have some more of that dried meat?" Koda looked toward Shane with her big brown puppy dog eyes, winning him over in an instant. He ripped off a piece of the jerky and threw it to her.

They ate nearly every bite of food. It was the first proper meal they had eaten since coming to this place. With full stomachs and a great sense of accomplishment they relaxed.

Trystan lay back on the warm stone; arms crossed behind his head, and stared up into the bright blue sky. He instinctually searched for Strix and when there was no sign of the evil creature, he let himself completely relax. He looked to his left and saw Koda stretching before them, lying on her side to catch a nap. He thought that was a great idea and knew she would alert him of any danger. Closing his eyes, the bright noonday sun shone on his face. He could feel his dark eyelashes getting warm, absorbing the heat.

Shane was happy. He was on his way to becoming a Tukki Tukki warrior. Removing his shoes and socks, with his staff in hand, he walked over to the water's edge. Sitting down he put his feet in the cool pool and sighed with how amazing it felt. He laid the staff over his lap and really took a good, long look at it.

It was a hard, darkened wood, smooth and shiny. It was engraved with the same runes that covered the prism's box and that had appeared on the stone door that had blocked the cave's entrance. He traced the design with his fingertips and felt the great magic that they possessed. Feeling warm and slightly dizzy, he held the staff with both hands and closed his eyes.

There was a flash, and in his mind appeared an image of his Aunt Greyson. She was smiling at him. The image slowly faded and Shane opened his eyes. He knew in his heart that she had seen him. It felt like she was nodding her approval. Being the one who inherited the Bo-staff, made him feel stronger. He stood and noticed that he was covered in sweat. He hated feeling hot and sticky and so he stripped down to his underwear and in his loudest voice shouted, "CANNONBALL!!!" He jumped into the air and made the biggest splash of his life into the waterfall's pool.

A wave of cool water crashed over Koda and Trystan, waking them suddenly from their warm naps, "AAAAgggghhhhh!!!!" The shout came from both of them at the same time.

"Oh that is it! You are in deep trouble now!" Trystan shouted as he stripped off his slime encrusted jeans, shirt, socks and shoes, diving into the pool after his brother. Koda shook the water from her fur and then happily jumped into the lagoon to have a swim with her boys.

The three of them played together and for a moment they forgot all responsibilities, their sadness, and fear. The two brothers and their pup just had fun. They splashed each other and played water tag. Climbing underneath the pounding waterfall they enjoyed the sensation of the water beating down on them. It was the coolest shower they had ever taken.

They washed their clothes at the far end of the pool, where the water got shallow and formed the mouth of the river. It didn't take them too long to scrub the slime and mud from their jeans, shirts, and socks. They swam them back over to the sunbathing rock and laid them out directly on the stone so they would dry. All three collapsed on the large blanket and stretched out, letting the hot sun warm them back up.

They felt alive. More alive than ever before.

CHAPTER 15

Koda was the first to stir among them. She stood and then stretched her front legs out as far as they would go, then her back legs extended out behind her one at a time. A loud howling yawn came from her mouth that woke the boys from their afternoon nap. She walked sleepily to them and got her scratches and belly rubs from each one, waking them up in the process. Trystan slowly stood and began to put his de-slimed clothes back on. Everything had dried nicely in the hot afternoon sun and was warm against his skin. He felt amazing, strong and re-energized.

As Shane began to dress, his brother looked over to him and asked, "Will you two pack up whatever food is left and refill our canteens? We need to be leaving here as soon as possible."

Shane nodded and began picking through the remains of their feast, wrapping up the leftovers, and placing them in his backpack. Koda made herself useful by dragging the canteens over to the pool but before filling them, was distracted by a fluttering butterfly dancing at the water's edge.

Trystan sat back down and grabbed his backpack. Opening the leather ties he saw the familiar pulse of the prism's box letting him know that there was new information available to them. Opening the prism was now second nature to him. He no longer had to use his hands for navigation and quickly used his mind to scan the *INDEX*. There was a new entry flashing under *TASKS*. He opened the folder and saw a new riddle had appeared.

Shane efficiently finished getting everything ready. After filling the canteens and attaching the Bo-staff to his pack, he entered into the prisms' orb to stand beside his brother. Koda, still distracted in her hunting of the butterfly, didn't join him.

High above the earth, where the Gatekeeper takes his rest
In the branches and the bramble, buried in his gruesome nest
Underneath the bones of prey that bloody feasts provide
An ancient firestone, stolen from the Guardians, doth lie
Be wary of the moment when the sun begins to set
Trapped in his domain at dusk will be your ultimate regret.

The boys stood there silently. Reading and re-reading the riddle they hoped that somehow it would say something different.

"It is talking about Strix isn't it Trystan." The calm feeling, he just had, slipped away with the mention of the wicked owl's name. Without thinking, Shane grabbed the Bo-staff pulling it free of its binding. Strength flowed from the staff up his fingertips, into his arm then throughout his entire body. It dulled the fear, but only a little bit.

"I'm afraid it has to be. He's the only one referenced as the Gatekeeper. Through the prism, I have seen his nest and the giant tree that it sits in. Just northwest of here." Trystan shook his head, knowing they had to find a way to outsmart Strix.

"So we have to sneak up into his nest and get some sort of stone? A firestone that was stolen from the Guardians?" Shane looked to his brother and Trystan nodded. "The Guardians? But Koda's a Guardian. Does that mean that there are more of them here?" Shane was confused. Could there be more of Koda's tribe around them?

Koda heard the boys talking, distracting her attention away from the butterfly. Hearing them mention the Guardians, she knew that it was time to share her story.

"I have something to tell you," she began, "Last night as I lay guarding the entrance to the cave, a voice called out to me. It was a voice that was familiar and echoed in my heart."

She told her boys of how she had been called down to the sunbathing rock where she met Emiko, an older Guardian who had been the one to save her from the young, hungry, and vicious Vargen that had her trapped long ago. She shared with them her knowledge of Ryker and the Guardians of the Day and Night who protected these lands. She described how they could communicate without speaking, instead with shared images in their minds. Finally, she told of how Emiko had been the one to bring her into Trystan and Shane's world.

After she shared her story, Trystan looked back at the prisms index and saw that it had been updated with the information for the Guardians and the Vargen. The power of this crystal continued to amaze him.

"Do you think if you called to them, with your mind like Emiko showed you, that they would come and help us get their firestone back?" Shane asked his little pup, hope lingering in his voice.

"It's possible but I don't know, I have never tried it." Koda replied.

"We're going to need all the help we can get if we're going to get that firestone from Strix. Once we get closer and get a plan together, would you try to call out to them?"

Trystan squatted down and looked Koda in the eye. He reached out his hand and pet her soft reddish fur along her back and her soft velvet ears. She leaned into his hand soaking in the love he extended.

"Of course I will, I would do anything for you two." Koda licked Trystan's hand, "We should get going, the sun is still high and that should give us plenty of time to make it to Strix's nest before he starts heading back for the night."

"I agree Koda. C'mon guys, let's go." Trystan closed the prism and put it away safely in his pack. Putting it on, he looked around at the beautiful lagoon and soaked in as much of the calmness surrounding him that he could. He wondered if they would ever see this place again.

Trystan knew there was danger ahead of them and that the help of the Guardians could be the difference between life and death.

CHAPTER 16

Koda led them away from the waterfall, past the cave of the Sacred Stone door, and down the trail where Arion had disappeared. They had all changed so much from when they had first come to this world. They were no longer frightened, young, and inexperienced. Trystan stood taller as he walked, with more confidence. He was starting to see that being different from his brother could actually be a good thing. Knowing Arion trusted him with the prism meant more than words ever could.

Looking ahead at his little brother, Trystan enjoyed watching him practice swinging his Bo-staff through the air with big sweeping motions over his head, then quick jabs forward and backward tucking it under his armpits. Improving with every motion, it was as though the staff's magic had awakened the warrior within Shane. The more he practiced, the more it seemed second nature. As he interacted with it he seemed to almost be downloading technique through his hands and muscles. It was more than a weapon. It was a tool that also contained the sacred magic of the Tukki Tukki.

Inspired, Trystan reached into his back pocket and pulled out the slingshot. The Battle of the Booslaaks had been really good practice for him but they moved slowly. He felt he needed to be better. Picking up random smaller rocks, he started looking around the forest ceiling for a target. It wasn't long before he spotted large white flowers high up in the trees' canopy. Hanging just below the leaves, these enormous puffs had hundreds of long petals that hung down like Pom-Poms.

Stopping on the trail, he took aim at a flower closest to him. It was about twenty-five feet up and a few yards to his right. Raising the slingshot, he took aim and fired. The small stone zipped through the air and caught the very edge of the flower. A few petals came loose and floated to the ground like falling snow. He took another stone and aimed again. Before letting it fly, he took a deep breath in and held it. Finalizing his aim, he released his breath and then let go. POP!!! The flower exploded like a firework, white petals cascading thought the air and decorating the forest floor.

Shane whizzed around after hearing the pop just in time to catch the petal explosion. "Cool! Do it again Tryst!"

Koda barked in agreement, "Yeah! I missed it, do it again!"

Trystan smiled, "Ok! OK! Which one? Pick one out."

Koda and Shane scanned the trees, there were plenty of options but it couldn't be too easy. Koda found one and pointed it out to Trystan.

"That one way up there?" Lifting his finger, he singled out a puff that was even higher than the last one.

"Yep! You can do it!" Koda was so excited she chased her tail for a few spins before stopping in a sudden sit.

He took his slingshot and placed a rock in the leather pouch before pulling it back. A deep breath in, he zeroed in on the flower, a breath out and release. POW!! The flower burst like confetti in a multitude of shreds. The focus he used when shooting his slingshot was similar to when he was using the prism.

"That was awesome!" Koda ran and rubbed against his leg.

"Thanks little bear." Trystan said, reaching down and scratching her ear. He knew his aim was getting better and it was nice to be able to help in their defense. "We should keep moving. We'll stay west on this trail for quite a while along the front of the mountains. We still have a lot of land to cover before we get to Strix's nest."

"Follow me!" Koda said as she bounded away, hopping like a small goat down the trail.

They continued on their way. Soon the trail widened into a broader path and all three of them could walk alongside one another. Shane continued to practice with his staff while Trystan was becoming more accurate exploding the Pom-Pom flowers as he walked. Koda was busy sniffing the air constantly searching for anything that would harm or help them. Her little radar ears were listening and always alert.

For over an hour they traveled this way. Stopping only to sip some water from the canteens or to catch their breath for moment or two. Their lunch had been big enough that none of them were hungry. They decided to continue on before they would need to stop for a quick snack.

The path began to narrow into a thinner trail and started to head up a large hill. The boys began to feel an ache in their leg muscles as they climbed. It started to get steep and the land was littered with bigger rocks. The trees were thinner and the ground was bare except for some small ferns that were scattered randomly throughout the area. Sometimes the trail wound around the larger boulders before snaking its way further up the mountain. Their pace was much slower now and they began taking water breaks more frequently. They knew they would need to find more soon or they would run out.

Almost reaching the top of the hill, Koda stopped, ears forward and listened with her whole body. The boys froze and stood silent allowing Koda to hear more clearly.

"What is it girl?" Shane asked as he crept quietly to her side, Bo-staff held tight.

"Someone or something needs help. They sound scared." She took a few steps closer, "But, I can't really tell, we are too far away."

"Let's move to the top of the hill, hopefully we can get a better view of what's going on. I'll look at the prism while you two scout it out, but be careful. I don't want to lose you." Trystan placed his hand on Shane's shoulder, "Either one of you."

"Got it, and don't worry we will. Right Koda?" Shane looked to his sidekick and she nodded.

They ran to the top of the hill and found a hiding spot behind one of the large stones half buried in the earth. Trystan squatted down and pulled out the prism while Shane and Koda began to sneak closer to the cries for help. They were now working as a team, each more comfortable with their roles.

Shane moved stealthily through the forest with Koda at his heels. Coming to the crest of the hill, they could see a small clearing at the bottom. The trail emptied out onto a grassy patch surrounded by the thick forest on one side and a 50ft rock wall on the other. The noises were coming from the bottom of the canyon. It sounded like someone was trapped.

"We should get a little closer Koda. Can you hear anything? Smell anything?" Shane was crouched behind a fallen tree trunk, its roots system weaving between earth and air.

A strong breeze suddenly made its way up the canyon and swirled around the two of them, carrying on its back the scents from below. The first color that filled Koda's nose was a bright yellow, but it was drenched in fear. She had detected it before, recently. Her mind worked quickly and in moments she recognized that it was from the Jibbetts. There was definitely more than one of those silly creatures down there.

There was also a second scent, a dark orange smell that made her hairs stand on end. She closed her eyes and through her nose inhaled deeply when her mind was overrun with images from her past. Memories that she had blocked for so long came rushing back like floodwaters. Back to the time she was the one trapped against a large tree, terrified, and her nose was filled with that same heavy orange scent.

It was the scent of the Vargen.

Chapter 17

Koda shook the fear from her mind. She knew that she must now come face to face with her ancient enemy and save those ridiculous little Jibbetts. She looked to her left and felt a surge of bravery as her young warrior stood by her side, Bo-staff in hand, and ready to go to battle.

"Follow me, there are Jibbetts and I smell Vargen," she whispered to Shane as she quietly crept her way down the trail toward the danger below. The bright yellow, fear drenched scent of the Jibbetts grew stronger as they made their way down the pathway. It was heavy in her nose and it made her feel angry with the Vargen for making these little creatures so terrified. Even though she had growled and chased them for throwing nuts at them, she would have never hurt them.

Shane followed the little guardian as quickly as he could. He felt like a ninja sneaking up on the enemy. He was also beginning to feel his adrenaline building up in preparation for the encounter. Reaching the base of the canyon, they found a large boulder to hide behind to plan their attack.

"I see two Vargen pinning the Jibbetts against that rock." Shane continued, peeking from behind the large stone, "I think that if I go running in on the attack, shouting and swinging my staff around, I could distract the Vargen long enough that you could run in and save those little rascals. What do you think?"

"I think that could work. I just don't know how easy it will be for me to convince them that I am trying to save them, and not eat them as well." Koda spoke in a low rumble. "What if the Vargen aren't that easily frightened?"

"We have to be brave and at least try. I know Jibbett's can be annoying Koda, but they don't deserve to be a Varg's lunch."

"You're right Shane. Let's save them!" Koda puffed out her chest with pride knowing that they were about to help someone who needed them.

Trystan felt uneasy as Koda and Shane crept down the trail, further away from him. The map was now displayed and he could see the bottom of the canyon where his brother and Koda were headed. Zooming in, he saw that there were three Jibbetts trapped against the canyon wall by two smaller Vargen. One Varg, larger than the other, was moving closer to the Jibbetts, pacing back and forth in front of them, getting closer with each step.

He watched the map's live feed and noticed that his brother and Koda had stopped behind a large rock at the base of the canyon about 100 feet behind the Vargen. He knew that they had come up with a plan. He could sense it. That's when he saw something that made his palms start sweating.

On the far edge of his map he saw three more Vargen closing in on the canyon basin. Koda and Shane could fight off two of them, but not five. Zooming out of the map, he estimated that they were about five hundred feet away and he needed to do something to distract the other three and keep them from joining their pack.

Down the trail, there was a large rock he could climb for an advantage against them. Knowing he didn't have time to overthink it, he quickly put the prism away, closed up the pack, and pulled out his slingshot. Taking a deep breath, he began running down the trail towards the boulder.

He flew down the canyon's sloping hillside, his feet keeping him steady as he made it to the large stone. Climbing to the top of it wasn't easy. Only after a few slips, he made his way to the top and sat, slingshot drawn, waiting for the remaining Vargen to appear over the ridge.

Shane and Koda looked at each other and knew that the time had come to put their plan into motion. Shane closed his eyes and grabbed his Bo-staff tightly with both hands. He felt the surge of its power rush through him as he prepared to face these terrible wolf-like creatures. He glanced over to Koda and saw that her Mohawk was back, running along the ridge of her spine, signaling that she too was ready.

As they stepped out from behind the boulder, Shane began running full speed towards the Vargen. Koda crept to the rock face quietly making her way to the Jibbetts. Shane let out a warrior's shout as he raised his staff high over his head.

"Aaaaaaaahhhhhh!!!!!" He screamed closing the distance between them.

The Vargen spun around to face the charging warrior, startled by this sudden attack. The larger of the two held his ground, eyes wide and teeth bared, as the smaller cowered behind his comrade. While Shane had them distracted, Koda arrived at the three Jibbetts. They were shaking in terror, tears streaming from their oversized eyes, and clinging to one another.

"Hurry, climb on," She spoke quietly and calmly. "I am Koda of the Guardian Tribe, a friend. I am here to save you. You have to trust me. We don't have time!!" The Jibbetts didn't move, frozen in place by their fear.

"Climb on my back, NOW!!" Koda barked at them. Quickly climbing up, they wrapped their tiny fingers in her fur and held on for dear life. She ran like the wind up the trail to where they had left Trystan. Everything in her hated leaving Shane alone with those predators, but she knew she needed to get the Jibbetts to safety quickly.

Shane ran towards the first Varg and swung his staff toward the beast's head. Its glowing red eyes flashed in anger, as saliva dripped from its snarling fangs. The Varg's jaws snapped loudly. His teeth crashed together, accompanied by a fierce growl, as he tried to bite the staff. The black fur bristling all over his body. The smaller Varg stood back, scared of this human creature. He wanted to run, to flee, but knew he couldn't leave his leader for fear of being banished from ever returning to the Shadowlands.

As the larger of the two Vargen kept his eyes on Shane, he knew that soon the rest of his pack would catch up. They should be coming over the ridge at any moment. If he could just keep this human child engaged long enough for them to get there, they would easily overpower him. Lunging at the boy, he was surprised by the quickness of this young human child. Shane took a step closer and felt the power of the Tukki Tukki flowing through his staff.

Swinging it with all his might, he connected to the side of the Varg and sent the brute rolling through dirt. A dust cloud rose up around them. Shaken, the Varg stood then lowered his head, growling and bearing his fangs at the young warrior.

Taking a step closer, Shane spoke directly to them. "I am Shane of the Tukki Tukki tribe. You aren't welcome here in this valley. We offer our protection to those who need it, including those Jibbetts that you were about to eat."

"Tukki Tukki...," the larger of the two Vargen spoke under his breath, "It can't be." Then raising his voice, spoke to Shane, "I am Obsidian Everbleed, youngest son of the Varg leader, Rogue Everbleed. It is you, child, that doesn't belong here. You have stumbled into OUR territories, and for that we will spare no punishment for you or your kind."

Obsidian stared directly at Shane while his ears listened for the rest of his pack. He had heard stories passed down from his father, and his father before him, about the Tukki Tukki. They were said to be surrounded by a powerful magic, but this one was small and alone. When his mates arrived, he believed they could easily take him down and return home to the Shadowlands as victors. Bringing back that Tukki Tukki staff to his father would prove his strength and leadership.

As the Vargen and Shane were engaged in a standoff, Koda reached the top of the trail and followed Trystan's bright blue scent down to the large boulder he sat perched on.

"You will be safe here with Trystan," she spoke gently to the Jibbetts who were still shaking with fear, "I will be right back. Shane needs me."

The little creatures slowly slid off Koda's back and huddled against the giant stone, arms wrapped tightly around each other. Koda wanted to get back to Shane but needed to touch base with Trystan first.

"Tryst, are you ok?" She called up to him and he peeked over the edge of the Boulder.

"Great job Koda," he responded. "I'm fine. There are more Vargen over there. I will try to distract them. Now go get Shane, and hurry before they get there first!" Koda wasted no time and headed down to the base of the canyon where her warrior faced the evil Vargen alone.

Trystan looked around. He needed to keep the other three Vargen from reaching the two below. He quieted the Jibbetts, who were still whimpering quite loudly, by offering them some of the nuts that were left over from their lunch. He peered out again over the landscape, eyes searching for the black pelts of their enemies. Seeing movement out of the corner of his eye, three blackened shapes appeared slinking down into the canyon. Smaller than he originally imagined, he felt his confidence grow.

He waited for them to pass through a clump of trees and into a clearing. As they crossed the last of the trees, he pulled back his slingshot and focused on the one in front. There was no room for error. Focusing his concentration, breathing in, taking aim, and releasing while letting his breath out, he let the ammo fly. Watching as the small stone hit its target directly on the nose, the small Varg yelped in pain and confusion as it fell to the ground. The two that had been following him looked around for their attacker. Not seeing anything, they did not want the same fate to fall upon them, so they grabbed their injured friend, and drug him back up the hill away from danger.

Trystan stood atop the boulder and in his loudest voice shouted, "WE ARE TUKKI TUKKI!" His voice echoed off the canyon walls and to the standoff below. Obsidian and his companion heard the yelp of one of their own, followed by the shout of a second human child. How many were there? He could not answer, so he signaled for retreat.

Turning he looked Shane directly in the eye. "Until next time young warrior!" Obsidian warned, "And when our paths cross again, I will be ready for you." The two Vargen turned to make their way out of the canyon the same time that little Koda came running to Shane's side.

"TUKKI TUKKI!!" Shane shouted, thrusting his Bo-staff in the air over his head. Koda threw her head back in a victorious howl, joining in the celebration. "We did it!" She cheered.

"Woo Hoo!! We did!" Shane agreed excitedly. Trystan heard the resounding cry and knew that signified a victorious end.

The conquered Vargen made their way back to their lair, heads down and tails between their legs. Approaching the entrance, a large shadowy figure emerged, nearly four times larger than any one of them. Obsidian raised his eyes to meet the smoldering stare, shame dripping from his fur as he spoke.

"Master, the Tukki Tukki, they have returned."

CHAPTER 18

Trystan looked up at the sun trying to decide what time it was. Judging by its placement in the western sky he assumed it must be 5:00, maybe 6:00pm. It was just above Strix's nest that was clearly still a good hours walk away. He figured they had about two or maybe three hours left before the sun would set. Possibly giving them just enough time to get there, get the firestone, and then get out before Strix returned.

His thoughts were broken by the Jibbetts chatter. They were looking down the path, pointing, jumping up and down. Glancing over Trystan saw Shane and Koda returning with big smiles on their faces. Trystan waved and smiled back. Shane, holding the center of his Bo-staff in one hand, raised it high above his head and gave it a couple victorious pumps into the air. Koda's attention was focused on the three jumping Jibbetts.

"Koda, oh Koda! Hero!" said one

"She comes! Hail Koda!" exclaimed another.

The third Jibbett said nothing but instead ran to greet Koda, arms filled with flowers, and one by one, lay the flowers on the ground in front of her as she walked.

Koda looked down as her paws experienced what it felt like to walk on flower petals for the first time. When she raised her head, she glanced over to the boys with uncertainty. They both smiled and nodded with pride. Koda's shyness went away as she tossed her shoulders back and held her head high. Gathering around her, the Jibbetts were abuzz with chatter and praise. Koda spoke back to them with respect and kindness. These little annoying things were not so annoying anymore. She loved being adored.

"You comes with us, meet Drey. Drey meet Hero!"

Koda got very excited about meeting a large amount of these creatures that she felt would all treat her the same way. Caught up in the adoration she began to say, "Sure," when Trystan interrupted.

"Sorry guys but we can't. We have just enough time to get the firestone from Strix's nest before nightfall."

The Jibbetts stopped talking, as their already big eyes grew even larger and their jaws dropped.

"Crazies!?" replied the first Jibbett who was clearly the one that spoke the most. "Jokes? No one to Strix's nest, NO ONE."

"Well we are!" Shane spoke clearly with growing bravery. "We have to go get something that Strix took away from the Guardians."

The Jibbetts turned and started chattering to each other in an unknown language. After a quick discussion of chatters, clicks, and squeaking sounds they turned said, "We go!" And off they ran.

Trystan and Shane looked at each other completely confused, shrugged their shoulders, and started walking in the direction of Strix's nest. Koda watched as the Jibbetts ran off. Her mouth turned down and she was surprised by her disappointment as she watched them disappear through the forest.

"Koda, come on girl," she heard Shane call to her.

During the hour walk to the nest, Trystan explained his plan. Shane would climb the tree as Trystan and Koda kept watch for Strix. Shane was very quick and a great climber so Trystan knew it was possible for him to get up there and back down quickly. He explained to Shane that he needed to listen closely for Koda's howl. It would alert him that Strix was spotted and that no matter what he needed to immediately start climbing down the second he heard it.

Shane's brow furrowed deep in thought as he prepared himself for this task. It would definitely be the most dangerous thing he had ever done. He was an excellent climber though. His mom used to take him to her gym when he was little. There was a rock-climbing wall and kids could take a class with a trained climbing instructor. He had mastered that wall and could go up and down faster than any of the kids, even the older ones. He began to envision himself climbing up the tree. Each time he thought of Strix though, the hair on his arms stood on end. He would just have to be fast.

In order to get his mind off of his nervousness, Shane started telling Trystan about the Vargen and exactly what had happened, including the warning Obsidian had given them. He had said they would meet again. Shane had no doubt the Varg had meant it, but he could not worry about that now. His mind shifted back to the task ahead of them.

Trystan, knowing they were almost to the large tree that housed Strix's nest, focused once again on the plan. While Shane was climbing, Trystan would use the prism to track Strix's location. As soon as he would enter its coverage area, Koda would howl and Shane could climb down with plenty of time. That also meant he would need to use the prism at the same time to find a place to seek shelter. One that would be safe and sturdy enough to protect them, yet close that they could escape to it in time. Most importantly, if they were anywhere near Strix they had to remain out of sight and absolutely quiet.

A couple of years ago, Trystan had to do a presentation in class and he chosen owls as his subject. He knew that they used their keen hearing ability to identify the precise location of prey they were hunting. Owls were also supposed to be nocturnal and sleep during the day. Strix hunted during the day and was clearly not anything like the owls Trystan had studied. He was becoming aware that things in this world were not always what one would assume them to be. He wondered what else he didn't know about Strix and shuddered at the thought of finding out.

Never in a million years would he have guessed he would actually use the information from his report, especially in a situation of life or death. *Did he just think that?* He didn't want to, but yes, this was indeed a life or death situation. It seemed like everything in this world was.

Trystan looked over at Koda and Shane and saw them looking up into the treetops. They clearly were studying something. Quickly looking up, he saw the fascination. He could not believe how big the nest was, the size of a large carousel, similar to the one that he rode on every year at the state fair.

"Come on you guys we are almost there," Koda spoke trying to hurry them.

Snapping back into reality, the two boys followed their little dog into the thick tall trees which created a wall shielding them from seeing the nest or any part of the very large tree housing the owl's lair. They had to keep on a straight path in order to find it. Knowing it was only about 50 yards in, and massive, it would be much bigger than the surrounding trees.

Koda ran ahead certain she could locate it. Within minutes she returned. "I found it!"

"Good job Koda! Come on guys we need to hurry. With these trees so thick blocking the sky, it will be hard to tell what time it is or how dark. We need to make sure we do not waste any time."

Trystan didn't want to tell them that he had reservations about his plan because it, in his opinion, was risky. The tree was much bigger than he expected. Figuring that they had, at the most, two hours before Strix would be headed back their way, he knew that they all would have to perform their part of the task perfectly. There was no room for error. Shane would only have thirty minutes to reach the nest and retrieve the stone. They would be cutting it very close.

No matter what amount of planning that he did, things were about to turn out differently. Very.

Chapter 19

As they approached the tree, it looked just like the prism had promised it would. It had a ton of branches that started very low. Shane knew he would definitely be able to climb it. Trystan would just need to hoist him up to get the first branch so he could begin.

Breaking the silence of the forest, the three heard a rustling behind them and a pitter-patter of many little feet coming toward them. Flipping around they stood frozen as the noise became louder. They could see the lower brush rustling just in front of them. The three little Jibbetts they had saved from the Vargen popped out into the clearing and about 25 more emerged from behind them, it was the entire Drey of Jibbetts!

"Hiyas!" The talkative Jibbett announced.

"What are you doing here little guys?" Shane spoke, relieved to see them.

With a huge smile on her face Koda stepped forward. On point, the Jibbetts fell to one knee bowing before their hero. "Hail Koda, Hero!"

Koda stood with pride. "Please rise. You really don't have to do that."

"We do, we do. Respects the Koda!"

Koda nodded as the Jibbetts rose to their feet.

"Drey knows of Koda, wants to help Tukki Tukki." The muscular Jibbett faced the others and lifted what looked like a mini samurai sword into the air exclaiming loudly, "Whatnee Hoich!" An additional twenty held up their swords, "Whatnee Hoich!" The twenty little voices cried out in unison. This clearly was their salute in the Jibbett Language.

"You has plans?"

"Shane is going to climb the tree to get the firestone that is hidden somewhere in the nest. Koda and I are going to watch for Strix and look for shelter. Strix will be back soon," Trystan explained to the Drey.

"Okays," the muscular Jibbett leader nodded his head. "You's five up tree with boy, rest stay with Hero!"

"Okay let's go!" Shane spoke holding up his Bo-staff and then handed it to his brother. "I won't be able to climb with this, so take good care of it."

Trystan was moved at this gesture, as well as impressed with Shane's focus and bravery. He had to admit, he was really glad he wasn't the one going up there. Taking the young warrior's new and most valuable possession, he held it tight.

"I will Shane. I promise." Holding his fist in the air, Shane immediately responded with a fist bump. "Good luck," Trystan looked at him with pride. The two stared at each other for a long moment. They knew they had to completely trust one another.

"Hey I want a fist bump too," Koda exclaimed as Shane gave a little tick on her paw. Then he stood up straight and looked up the giant tree while tightening the straps on his pack to make sure it was secure.

"Come on then, I will lift you. Put your foot in my hand, then you can reach the first branch." Shane did as his brother asked. Trystan was tall and strong enough to lift him. Before he knew it, he was up on the first branch reaching up to continue to the second.

Koda and Trystan watched as Shane climbed up the great tree, with the Jibbetts following right behind him. Shane moved quickly through the dense branches. There were many limbs, so maneuvering up was rather easy. He also knew that if he slipped, his fall could easily be broken, which made for a quick, confident climb.

As Shane navigated his way up, Trystan looked over at the remaining Jibbetts who stood, some staring at him, as the others adored Koda. They were petting her fur and bringing small gifts to lie at her feet. They weren't very smart but they were pretty funny, and they ran really fast. If he could find potential places to hide, they could divide up and go check them out.

Trystan put down his backpack and took out the prism. Opening it up easily, he realized how quickly this was becoming normal to him. Turning to look at the Jibbetts, he asked a few of them to stay with Koda and watch Shane. Their job would be to alert those climbing when Strix was coming. Eagerly the chosen few took great honor in helping their hero, Koda.

Trystan explained to the remaining Jibbetts he would require their help to seek out a safe place to hide once Shane returned. They would need to use their quickness and navigation skills to check out the identified spots.

"Do you guys think you can do that?" he asked, hoping they were better at finding their way around than they were at figuring things out.

"Good at things! Finding things!"

"We's are?" several Jibbetts said in unison looking around at each other blankly, completely confused. Trystan began to look worried.

"Well, we's are," the smart looking Jibbett said and pointed to himself and to three others. Trystan had to admit that they didn't have the empty carefree look in their eyes that the three they had saved did. He wasn't trying to be mean; it was just his observation. He opened up the prism and, as the orb materialized around him, the Jibbett's let out a great chorus of awe. Trystan giggled to himself at their response.

"Okay you four. Help me scan this map for something that looks like it might be good shelter. Then one by one, I will send you to check it out. But first the rest of you, I need you to keep a close eye out for a very large moving object that will be in the sky." Trystan pointed to the area of the prism where Strix would appear. "That will be Strix. When you see him, let me know immediately, then we can alert Koda. She will howl at Shane so he can make it safely down before Strix gets back to his nest. Clear?"

"Clear as sky!" one Jibbett announced. Trystan looked up. There was an umbrella of branches everywhere, definitely no sky in sight. He knew he had better keep his eye on both tasks since he had a hard time trusting others to do a thorough job. He liked to do things a certain way, his way.

Trystan scanned the prism once more for Strix and saw nothing. The surrounding area also brought up no large living creatures or movements, so he figured at least for now all was good. Diverting his attention, he went back to focusing on the map with the four scholarly Jibbetts.

Almost to the top of the tree, Shane and the Jibbetts were climbing at lightning speed. They were fast and so was he. He giggled as one or two passed him and he could look up and see their bushy tails swinging behind them as they moved. As one Jibbett passed he let out a loud belch.

"Excuuuuuuuuussse ME," the little creature announced.

Shane giggled, fanning his face for a moment. "Gross, that stinks. Have you been eating poop or something?"

"Poop food!" said the Jibbett then rushed ahead. Shane scrunched up his nose. He was impressed that the Jibbett had accomplished the impossible. He was completely grossed out.

Refocusing, they soon emerged through the ceiling of branches and leaves to reveal just twenty yards higher, the giant mass. Strix's nest was built of large tree branches, some smaller younger tree trunks stripped of their branches, and different kinds of brush and bramble. Looking at it this closely, it really was a work of art.

Approaching the top where the nest lay woven in the giant limbs of the tree, Shane had not thought about how he would actually get into the nest. It looked so tightly constructed, that it seemed impossible for him to find a way through. Shane and the Jibbetts had all stopped at the base of the nest with nowhere further to climb.

In frustration, Shane said, "Aw, man. Now what?"

The strong Jibbett moved up to the top, pulled out his sword and said, "Duh duh da!!" The other Jibbetts followed and soon their swords were cutting into the leaves and sticks creating a tunnel through the bottom of the nest. Just big enough for them to all fit through one by one.

Shane was last and he pulled himself up through the final layer of Strix's nest. It hadn't been easy, and he had definitely scraped his stomach on a stick that was poking out. He could feel the burning as he lifted up his shirt revealing a scratch that was glowing red. Luckily, there was no blood.

Looking around, he saw the nest floor was littered with bones of all shapes and sizes, as well as jet black feathers from the enormous owl. He reached down and picked one up. The feather was almost as long as his arm. He quickly took off his pack and placed it inside as he continued searching the nest. There was no sign of the firestone. He knew it must be hidden within the nest itself. As he looked to the sky, he saw the sun hadn't set, but it wouldn't be long. Directing his attention to the northern facing side of the nest, he saw all the Jibbetts lined up and looking out at something. Walking over, he began to climb up to see out over its edge. He was very curious about what they were looking at that seemed to captivate their attention.

Pulling himself up and standing with the others, his mouth dropped open. What he saw in the distance filled him with as much wonder as it did terror. He couldn't believe his eyes!

While they stared out at this mysterious place, they were completely unaware that an enormous flying object had entered the prism's radar. Down below, as of yet, no one had noticed it.

CHAPTER 20

Trystan had been very busy scanning the map, identifying what looked like a potential shelter. He saw a large hole in the side of a hill just on the outskirts of the forest, so he sent a Jibbett off to have a look. He saw a large tree with high roots that seems to have a hidden hole underneath. Again he sent another Jibbett out. Being so focused on the tiniest of details in the map, he did not see the large mass begin to enter the radar. The Jibbetts, that were supposed to be looking out for Strix, were very busy watching Trystan, as well as tracking each Jibbett that was on the search. They had entirely forgotten their task.

Several minutes after the bird had entered the radar, Trystan glanced over at the other Jibbetts and panicked when he saw they were actually watching him. Moving his attention to the sky area of the map, he was shocked to see they had all missed Strix. He was flying directly for them. Though he was probably a couple miles away, he knew it would not take long to be within range of hearing them near and in his nest.

"Koda quick, its Strix! Starting howling! Alert Shane!" Trystan had learned that if he concentrated enough, he could still keep the prism open while directing his attention outside of its realm.

Koda who was on high alert anyway, immediately sat up and let out a loud howl, several shorter ones, and then an even louder long one. Trystan immediately stared at the top of the screen where he could see the movement in the sky. It was getting closer. Shifting his attention to the nest, he could see the figures were not moving down the tree. He realized at that moment they couldn't hear Koda that far up in the treetop.

"They can't hear you Koda!" Trystan felt a deep terrified feeling began to drop to the pit of his stomach as his heart raced. What could he do? Koda looked down at the Jibbetts surrounding her.

"Go tell them to get down immediately. Hurry, there isn't time!"

Koda, Trystan and the remaining Drey watched their comrades scurry quickly up the tree. This time faster than the ones before, who had slowed their pace to stay with Shane. But these guys could really go full throttle.

Trystan kept a close eye on Strix. He was moving even closer now, maybe just a few hundred yards away. Glancing back up the tree, he was just in time to see the Jibbetts break through the umbrella of branches. They were almost there.

Koda was very worried and knew that it was time to call to her tribe just like Emiko had explained. Closing her eyes, she began to see herself talking to Emiko by the water. She felt how Emiko was able to speak to her. A tingling sensation began to develop in her paws. Moving up her legs, through her body and out through her forehead, her thoughts began to emerge.

"Emiko, we need your help. We need all of you. It is Strix and he is close. Shane is in grave danger. Please come." Koda could not believe the feeling of calm that swept through her body and it was only then that Emiko responded.

"We are here Koda. We always have been. We have been waiting for you to use your power."

At the close of her thought, the Guardians began to emerge from behind her. She immediately recognized Emiko. Beside Emiko, Koda saw another familiar face, one from long ago. It was Ryker. Her father.

In the large nest Shane stood mesmerized with his new friends looking out over the great expanse of the land. The wind blew across them, cooling the sweat that poured from Shane's face. Looking out into the sky, he saw the sunset reds and yellows glowing. Scanning the vast land before him, he could still see for miles even though the sun was going down. The view was spectacular, he had never been so high up and what he saw took his breath away.

Just beyond the mountains he could see an expansive pasture with a few trees scattered throughout. Beyond that was a large body of water where the setting sun glowed making the waters shimmer like a sea of tiny crystals. Past the water were red rocks and boulders that had more of a desert look. The shadows of the dispersed trees reminded him of giant stick creatures. It looked more like the pictures he saw of Arizona or Nevada, lonely in its stark beauty. As his eyes continued to look beyond, he noticed something else far off in the distance. He could not quite make out what he was seeing though. It was a very large structure that had jagged edges and was shrouded in darkness. It gave him a chill that ran down his back, making him shiver.

Just then Shane heard something scurrying and yelling, from below the tunnel they created in the nest. "Do you hear something?" It sounded like Jibbetts. "Guys, what are they saying?" He turned to listen. "Wait, it must be Strix! Quick, let's find the firestone!" Shane looked up searching the sky, but could not see anything...yet.

Four more Jibbetts emerged from the nest tunnel and quickly started helping with the search. They were tripping and jumping over bones, scurrying in an uncontrolled fashion. Shane began to quickly scan the nest. He thought of his Bo-staff and the clarity he had when it was with him. Just thinking of it, helped him to have laser focus. On the other side of the nest, and very close to the tunnel where they had entered, something was glowing. It seemed to be reflecting the sun and immediately caught Shane's eye.

"There!" He pointed, jumping forward and moving with haste, he made it in five big steps. Squatting down, he tried to fit into the space inside the nest wall. He was too big so he reached through, arm extending as far as it could, but the glowing red stone was just beyond his grasp. He felt a Jibbett jump off his knee and slide through the space, easily grabbing the stone and returning it to Shane. With no time to inspect it, he shoved it into his pocket that was deep enough to protect it.

"Good job! Now let's go! You guys go first!"

The Jibbetts began to dive, one by one, through the tunnel easily. Shane moved his eyes from the sky to the only exit, waiting for his turn. In the distance, he could see Strix circling over the Sacred Stone Door. Shane thought to himself. *Strix has realized the cave entrance is now open. He will know we're here!*

As the last two Jibbetts ran through, Shane quickly began to squeeze into the tunnel. It was at that point he could hear the sound of Strix's enormous wings flapping in the wind, coming closer and closer. Shane sucked in his stomach that he had scraped earlier, slipping through more easily this time. With only his head still peeking out of the hole, he felt the wind created from the powerful wing movement above. The air rushed loudly around him, whipping debris and feathers past his face. Shane glanced up to see Strix's sharp talons coming in for a landing and extending out to grab him, an angry shriek filling his ears.

Shane slipped down through the hole just as the large talons crashed into the nest right above his head. Moving down the tree quickly, he looked up. He was just in time to see a huge, sharp beak digging through the bottom of the nest at the hole they had made, trying to make it even bigger. The Jibbetts were already making their way down the tree at high speed. The four that had gone up with Shane were staying with him as they did before. Shane's arms and legs had never moved so quickly. He was fully focused on getting past the umbrella of branches as fast as possible so he would be shielded from Strix's sight.

The great owl's beak chipped away at some of the branches making the hole slightly wider. Shane could feel bits of stick and brush hitting his arms, shoulders and the top of his head. He had to stay moving. Then he saw a shining light coming from above him, allowing him to see better and move even quicker.

Strix's eye was looking through the hole, providing the glowing beam. He was just in time to catch a glimpse of the human child with curly hair disappearing under the leaves and branches below. Strix shifted his attention to the firestone. He had to make sure it was still there.

It was gone! They had stolen the stone! Furiously launching himself from the nest, his eyes began glowing even brighter with his anger as a hate-filled cry echoed through the forest.

Below Shane was moving quickly but having difficulty seeing in the darkness of the leaves. Further below, Trystan, surrounded by the Guardians and Jibbetts, had gotten out his flashlight and was shining it upward into the tree, hoping in some way this would help Shane. There was an army of creatures all looking up, waiting to see movement. Koda sat beside Trystan nervously.

Trystan had already put the prism away in his backpack, which was secure on his back. He had only put it away once he saw Strix in his nest, and Shane moving down the tree. He knew it was time to gather the group to be ready for whatever was about to happen next. His plan was to get Shane down and then they would go to the hole in the hill. The Guardians had confirmed it was big enough to shield all of them away from Strix and be safe. Trystan hoped they would have the chance but he took precautions, just in case.

Along with the flashlight, he had gotten out his slingshot and put it in his back pocket. In his other hand, he held the Bo-staff for Shane. Even though they had an army, he wasn't sure they would be any match for Strix, when their only weapons were only a slingshot and a Bo-staff.

Looking up with the flashlight shining, Trystan was worried about his little brother. Suddenly they all heard a noise above them. Branches and leaves began lightly falling. Strix was wildly trying to get his big body through the protective layer of tree limbs. Trystan glanced up the tree, relieved he could now see Shane and the Jibbetts moving steadily closer to the ground. Trying to provide as much light as possible, his heart began racing even faster. Glancing from Shane to the top of the tree, Trystan was getting very nervous.

"Come on Shane, you can do it!" Trystan yelled.

Shane was moving as fast as he could. He could hear the enormous owl above him, as branches continued to fly to the ground past him. Mostly missing him, he was protected by the layers of branches that surrounded. He could finally see Trystan and Koda at the bottom and was glad Trystan had gotten out the flashlight. It helped him move faster. He also felt the security of the Jibbetts moving alongside. They were his team.

The Jibbetts were the first to hit the ground and the remaining Drey immediately surrounded them. Shane finally got to the last branch of the tree and jumped down, landing skillfully on both feet.

"Shane!" Trystan yelled, throwing him his Bo-Staff.

"Come on everyone, we need to go to the..."

Trystan could not get his sentence out before a loud cracking noise emerged from above. Large branches began to fall from the sky as the enormous owl came half flying, half tumbling down.

Landing just before them, Strix shook the forest floor with a powerful BOOM!

Chapter 21

The army watched Strix shake his head and stumble around, clearly disoriented. Trystan studied the creature very quickly. Even though it was almost dark, there was now a big hole in the top of the trees, and what little light was left came shining through. Trystan pointed his flashlight on him to get a good look.

He was beyond huge, gigantic actually, and standing right before them. It looked like there were pieces of branch sticking out of his body. Clearly, breaking through the branches had injured the great beast. Trystan handed his flashlight to the scholar Jibbett next to him. He had really grown fond of these few, and knew they could be trusted.

"Keep it shining on him," Trystan whispered.

He reached into his pocket and pulled out his slingshot. He drew back, aiming at the only part of Strix he thought he could injure, even if only slightly. His eye. His target was not as clear as he had hoped, but he fired anyway.

Missing, he hit Strix with a CRACK on his sharp beak. This seemed to awaken the large owl from his dazed state as he shook his massive head.

Looking directly over to the boys, the lights in his eyes began to glow. He was now fully aware of them and remembered his obligation. It was his duty to protect this land from the human children that would appear, and those creatures that pose a threat to the darkness. He also must retrieve the Firestone of the Guardians'. It was the key to him taking down their kind. He could not eat them without it.

The beam of brightness that came from his eyes immediately blinded everyone in its path. Squinting and shielding their eyes with their hands, the army could not see anything. They were only able to hear him. Boom! The ground shook. They could feel Strix's massive step shake the earth below them. CRASH! Sounds of snapping sticks and branches filled their ears.

An eerie silence fell across the forest as the blinded army waited.

Then slowly the lights moved over the boys and Strix's beak suddenly became visible, thrusting forward within inches of Trystan and Shane's face. SNAP! They could feel his hot breath wash over them. It smelled of death and rotted flesh. They couldn't believe that he had missed them. How did he miss them? Why were they still alive? These thoughts ran through all of their minds simultaneously as they watched the light of the predator's eye shift down behind him to his foot.

Again, his eyes were the lights revealing what prevented him from moving forward. Strix's left claw was entangled in the branches of an even larger piece of tree that was lying on the forest floor. It had come crashing down with him when he had landed. He must have stepped directly into it. His headlight eyes searched the trunk as he shook his foot, trying to free himself.

Trystan knew that this was their moment, the evil bird was compromised. This would be there one chance. Possibly the only one they would get.

"NOW!!!!" Trystan yelled louder than ever before. The Jibbetts and Guardians raced forward, starting to attack Strix's good leg. As the beast backed up to stand upright, he tried to free his foot by shaking it free of its snare. Batting them away with his massive wings, he sent several of them tumbling back in a swoop as another round of the army began to charge forward.

Strix bent over and picked up one of the guardians in his massive beak. Thrashing his head backwards, he flung it high into the air and out of sight. Reaching down again, he took a few Jibbetts in his monstrous jaws and began to munch on them crushing their bones easily. He was indeed very hungry and he intended on eating all of these tiny animals and the two human children. He would retrieve the Firestone and finally eat all of the Guardians too. His hunger would be satisfied for days.

Koda and her father charged into battle together. Side by side they ran towards their great enemy. Strix immediately recognized Ryker. He was the most powerful of the Guardians, and most certainly his greatest nemesis. This wasn't their first battle. He had come across him several times. The last being when he stole the Firestone from him. He turned his large body to face the onslaught and opened his bloody beak letting out a terrible shriek. Following her father's lead, Koda leapt at the enormous owl, her fangs bared. They bit down hard on his legs, Ryker on one, Koda on the other. The owl screeched in pain as he shook them free. They circled around for a second attack and when they got close enough they leapt into the air. With a powerful swipe of his wing, Strix sent the two Guardians flying backwards. Koda, letting out a loud yelp that crushed the boys' heart, smacked against a large tree as Ryker landed in the bushes just next to her. Shane and Trystan saw Koda laying there, not moving.

Horrified at the massacre and angry that Koda was hurt, Trystan once again raised his slingshot. With focused aim, he hit Strix hard, this time right in the blinding, yellow eye. The beast stumbled back again, the earth shaking with each footstep, as the Guardians and Jibbetts relentlessly continued to charge at Strix.

Turning to Shane, Trystan saw he had the Bo-Staff up and was focused directly on Strix. He had never seen his little brother have such concentration. The young warrior's sights were set on the evil murderous bird with great determination.

Shane had been busy the entire time getting the Bo-staff to do what it had done to the Booslaaks. After he looked and saw Koda wasn't moving, he directed his anger towards the owl and on attacking him. He began to channel all of that energy into the Bo-Staff.

Shaking and twisting his foot, Strix was finally able to free himself. Now he would be able to fight with full force and end the pitiful lives of the army that surrounded him. They would be no match for him. He spotted the smaller human child with curly hair who had stolen the Firestone from his nest. He would target him first and retrieve the stone. He would enjoy the taste of every crunching human child bone in his mouth. Shaking and swiping the Jibbetts and Guardians off of him to clear the path, Strix came within a few steps of Shane. The entire forest floor was a constant vibration as he moved forward.

Trystan looked from the owl to Shane again. In his head he was encouraging him but did not want to say anything aloud to break his concentration. His little brother had to do something with his weapon; there was nothing else that could save them at this point.

As the owl closed in with his second step, a powerful blue light shot from the end of the Bo Staff and smacked Strix directly in the chest knocking him backwards. Shane and his Bo Staff were on the attack with another powerful burst, even greater this time. Shane was fully focused. This pushed Strix back even farther.

Shane concentrated even harder. He thought of his little pup lying motionless, and with fury another burst came from the Bo Staff, this time at full power, smacking Strix hard on the chest. Twisting and tumbling, the beast fell back onto a large pointed branch that went right through the center of his body. After shaking and trembling, the monster became motionless. Trystan, slingshot still aimed at the giant bird, was not quite ready to celebrate. He remembered what had happened down in the Booslaaks' lair and didn't want to be caught off guard again. As he circled around the fallen predator, he saw the sharpened end of the stick covered with feathers and what appeared to be some blood. He took a careful step a bit closer. The eerie silence gave him the chills.

Suddenly, the giant bird's chest heaved, sucking in air before letting out a terrible screech of pain. He shook his body, twisting and shrieking trying to free himself. There was a loud SNAP! Strix stood teetering before them. He had broken free from the trunk, yet the branch still remained through his body.

A gasp came from the Jibbetts as they ran for safety up the trees and behind the growling Guardians. Shane and Trystan stood there bravely, weapons raised, facing the injured beast. Strix tried to take a few steps, his eyes closed in pain, weak from his injury. He lifted a giant claw and then fell hard to the ground, the weight of his body shaking the earth beneath them. Shuddering a few more times, their enemy lay unmoving. A few minutes passed before they lowered their weapons. The great bird was defeated.

The army cheered and began to celebrate as Trystan and Shane ran over to Koda. She was not moving.

CHAPTER 22

The boys ran to their small pup that had fought so bravely. She lay very still. Dropping to their knees, one on each side of her, they couldn't hold back the tears that were burning down their cheeks. Shane reached out to stroke Koda's face, being as gentle as he could.

"Koda," his voice cracked through the pain in his heart, "Koda, are you there? Please wake up." Gently he ran his finger up her snout, over her forehead and behind her ear. A tear ran down his nose and fell to the ground below. Trystan sat in disbelief staring down at their little Guardian. He placed his hand on her side and closed his eyes. He couldn't feel her breathing, or the beat of her heart. He shook his head slightly. He wouldn't accept it. She couldn't be gone.

The army had gathered, surrounding them. The Jibbetts, wailing and crying in sobs and chatters, clung to each other, as they saw their hero lying lifeless. The Guardians had formed a circle around them, all standing silently feeling the grief and loss of their fallen as well.

A howl from behind a large bush pierced the silence. The cracking of small branches and the swish of leaves in the bush next to them distracted them slightly. Ryker emerged limping, letting out a small cry with each painful step. The army opened up a path by stepping to the side, allowing him to pass through to the inner circle. Slowly he approached Koda, sniffing the air and searching for her life scent. He smelled only a trace of her once vibrant fuchsia essence and lowered his head closer to hers.

"Koda of the Guardians, today you have honored your tribe, acted in bravery, and gave the ultimate sacrifice," his deep voice spoke solemnly, "You have made me so proud." He gently kissed her forehead and backed away a few steps before raising his eyes to Trystan and Shane.

Shane reached into his pocket and pulled out the firestone taking one last look at it before shakily handing to Ryker. It glowed with a deep churning red light that swirled underneath its polished surface. As the guardian accepted the Stone he spoke to the boys.

"Trystan and Shane of the Tukki Tukki, on this day of great accomplishment and great loss, the Guardians are forever in your debt. You have returned to us the firestone that will keep our clan safe from the dark powers of those like Strix. I am deeply sorry for your loss. She will be remembered as a hero." Ryker slowly turned and walked to the outside of the circle, a few of the Guardians began to tend to his wounds, cleaning them and feeling for any breaks in his bones.

Trystan and Shane sat in silence, staring at Koda's still body. They had never known loss. The heaviness and sharp pain that surrounded their hearts was unbearable. Neither of them moved. They couldn't bring themselves to stand, keeping their hands resting on her soft fur.

Behind them the ground began to shake, heavy footsteps falling, and moving closer. The area around them began to glow, the inner circle filling with a warm soft light. Again the outer circle parted and this time it was mighty golden hooves that approached them.

Arion stood over the boys and lowered his mighty head. Not saying a word, his great silver horn became brighter and brighter. It's magic dripping all around them. He gently placed it on the top of Koda's head and spoke with great tenderness.

"Sweet little one, you are a mighty Guardian. You were very brave. This is not the end for you, it is not your time yet."

The horn flashed with a brilliant white and then faded back into its soft silver. Arion lifted his head and made eye contact with every Guardian and Jibbett that made up this mighty little army. He nodded at Ryker and Emiko, and they bowed before the majestic unicorn.

Below him, Trystan felt something move underneath his hand. Her heartbeat was there again and it was strong. All of a sudden, he felt the lungs of his little pup fill with air and she took a huge breath. As life entered back into Koda, a beautiful, silver marking appeared in her fur following the breath re-entering her body. The mark was a scrolling design, tribal in nature, that traveled from her left eye, along her side and up through the curl in her tail; forever a reminder that the unicorn's magic had brought the young Guardian back.

Shane and Trystan cried out in unison, "Koda!"

The little pup blinked her eyes a few times and took a few more deep breaths. She could feel the love of her boys flowing through their hands. Becoming aware of the pride that her father and the other Guardian's had in her, her strength continued to grow. In her ears she could hear the adoration from the Jibbetts, who were now all dancing and cheering around them, celebrating their Hero's return.

Weak, Koda stood to her feet. She was not broken. She took a step forward and realized she was not even injured. Arion's magic had completely healed her. She shook off the feeling of death and looked at her boys, without any hesitation she ran and jumped on them, licking their faces and their tears away. Shane scooped her up in his arms and snuggled her tight.

"We thought we'd lost you little Bear, I never want to lose you. You were so brave." He covered her head and face with kisses. She leapt from his arms and ran back over to Trystan who was crouched down on his heels. Koda stood on her hind legs, front paws on Trystan's shoulders and nuzzled into his cheek. He hugged his little pup and kissed her on the forehead.

"It is so good to have you back, I don't know what we would ever do without you. I am so proud of you; you truly are a Guardian."

Trystan stood and looked around. Forgetting himself, he ran to Arion and threw his arms around the muscular neck. The unicorn's eyes grew wide, it was rare for anyone to dare touch him, but he felt the child's gratitude and allowed it, wrapping his mighty head around Trystan's shoulders returning the gesture. Trystan thanked him over and over for bringing Koda back to them. Gathering his emotions, he turned to face all of the amazing creatures that made up their army, and felt thankful for every one of them. They would have never survived this without their help.

"Shane and I would like to thank you all," Trystan's voice became strong and clear. "Without your help, this victory would have been impossible. We are in debt to you and offer the protection of the Tukki Tukki to all of you." A cheer rose from the Jibbetts, and the Guardians bowed in response. Emiko approached them.

"The sun has almost set, we must gather our dead and take them to the burial grounds. We will then accompany you back to your cave. Even though Strix is with us no longer, there are still dangers that lurk in these forests at night. Follow me."

The procession that led from Strix's nest to the burial grounds was one of silence. Ryker and Emiko led the way, followed by the Guardians who now carried their three fallen comrades. Behind them came Trystan, Shane, and Koda, surrounded by the remaining Guardians. The Jibbetts ran along side and behind them quietly, showing respect for those who had sacrificed their lives in the battle.

Reaching a grassy area, the procession stopped and the three dead Guardians were laid side by side and then surrounded by those who remained. Ryker and Emiko stood next to one another and let out long howls into the night air. The rest of the Guardians, including Koda, joined in the woeful chorus, mourning the deaths of their companions. The boys and Jibbetts stood silently as they witnessed this sacred ritual. The silver moon broke through a patch of clouds, its moonbeams bathing the fallen warriors in a reverent light.

All of the Guardians took a few steps forward parting into three groups and began to dig into the earth, three separate graves. Koda, experiencing this for the first time, watched for a moment before stepping forward to join in. Trystan and Shane soon joined in as well, dropping to their knees and using their hands to dig as best they could. With the graves now dug, the burial ceremony continued as, one by one, the fallen Guardians were placed into their eternal resting place, and then covered with the loose earth.

Ryker's strong voice filled the silence. "Fallen Guardians, today you have passed into the Great Expanse through the highest form of bravery. Our victorious battle against Strix could not have been accomplished without your sacrifice. Sakota and Thane, brave Guardians of Night, and the fearless Askari of the Guardians of Day, you will be eternally remembered and honored." With that he let out a long howl, the sound of absolute sorrow, and was joined by the rest of the Guardian Tribe in their final farewell song.

Their cries echoed out of the clearing and were carried on the night breeze, through the forest, and beyond the canyon. The sound of the pain filled howls brought a sinister and satisfying smile to the snarling fangs of a very large Varg. His huge red eyes pulsated with an ancient evil as he soaked in the grief the Guardians expressed.

CHAPTER 23

After the burial, the Guardians that remained accompanied Trystan, Shane, and Koda on the journey back to their cave. Emiko informed them that Ryker had been taken back to the Guardians' Keep to be further treated for his wounds. Shane walked alongside Koda, while Trystan flanked Emiko's other side.

Not much was spoken the rest of the way. They stopped once for a brief moment to drink from the canteens, and eat some of the food that they had left. It was hard for them to eat, but they forced it down. Everyone was overwhelmed and exhausted from the battle against Strix. The distance was covered quickly and soon the army's scattered remnants made it back to the entrance of the cave. Emiko turned to look at the human children and the little Guardian.

"A few of my comrades and I will stay here and guard the entrance to the cave tonight. The three of you have had a very long and hard day. Go inside and get some sleep without fear or worry of danger. Know that you are protected." She made a few slow circles, then settled down at the edge of the platform looking out over the forest below.

Shane and Trystan slowly walked into the cave, followed by a few of the Jibbetts that had returned with them, including the three that they had saved. As Trystan removed his backpack and shoes he checked to make sure the key was around his neck. He was relieved to find it still there.

Shane began making a small fire to warm the cave, while Koda stayed out by Emiko's side for a while longer. There were a few things that she wanted to ask her while she had the time.

"Emiko, is Ryker, um I mean my father, going to be ok?"

The wise old Guardian turned and smiled at her.

"Yes little one, he will be fine. His injuries are not beyond our healer's knowledge or capability. You made us all very proud today, and what an amazing marking you now have." She said nodding towards Koda's beautiful silver marking.

Koda turned and looked herself, "Wow!! I hadn't even noticed! It is beautiful." Admiring her new mark and then turning to Emiko, she became very serious. "Was I dead?"

"No Koda, you were in the in-between. If you would have crossed into the Great Expanse, no amount of magic would have brought you back." Emiko then added, "Like Arion said, it was not your time."

"It was very quiet," Koda continued, "I felt like I was floating in a great darkness. I could hear the cries of Trystan and Shane. I was trying to find my way back to them, but couldn't. Then I saw a white light begin to glow, so I headed that way. The next thing I remember is waking up. Did magic leave this mark on me?"

"The great magic that called you back has indeed left its mark on you. You are special and have been chosen for great things. Now go, join your boys and sleep."

Koda stood and stretched, a long yawn escaping from her mouth. She walked proudly down the cave corridor into the large room in the back. The three Jibbetts had made themselves comfortable near the fire, and stood when she entered. She walked to them welcoming their affection, then told them to sleep.

It was much warmer back here and it began to make her eyes feel very heavy. She patted over to where Trystan had fallen asleep with his glasses still on. Gently, Koda placed them between her front teeth and pulled them off his face, then carefully set them underneath his cot. She gave him a few quick kisses before walking over to where

Shane lie, passed out on his back, with his Bo-staff still tightly grasped in his hand. Rubbing her back against his hand, he dropped it to the floor and absent-mindedly began scratching along the little pup's spine. She jumped up onto his cot, made a few quick circles, then lay, tucked against his side. Sleep found her quickly and soon all three were snoring heavily, lost in their dreams.

CHAPTER 24

Shane could feel the uneven bones beneath his feet and the rough branches below his hands, as he stood at the edge of Strix's nest. The wind whipped around him, loud in his ears. He could see for miles in any direction, the small field to the south, where they had come into this strange land, the waterfall and caves to the east, but what pulled at him was what he saw to the north.

There was a jagged outline of a shadowed stronghold of some sort. Black stone, and shards of crystalized stone jutted out of it at awkward angles. There was a heavy power attached to that place, he could feel its evil.

What kind of creature would live there? he thought. He wanted to get a better look, so he climbed further up the nest's edge and stood at the top, balancing carefully in the gusty breeze. As he focused, trying to see what lie ahead more clearly, the nest shook below him with a powerful force.

Twisting around, he saw that Strix had landed directly behind him and was very angry. They had stolen the firestone from him, and now he wanted revenge. His eyes blinded Shane with their bright beams of light. As Strix's terrible beak opened and snapped towards him, he lost his footing and fell backward from the top of the nest. Falling rapidly to the ground below, the owl's evil, blinding eyes peered out from over the edge and shone directly onto Shane.

Shane fell from his cot to the dirt floor, covered in sweat. Koda, who had been sleeping next to him was also now on the floor, confused and startled. She was bristled up, her hair standing on end and she was staring at him. The three Jibbetts, who had snuggled up to them in the night, had been flung through the air when Shane fell off his bed, and were now in a tumbled heap chattering angrily at each other. They ran off and out of the cave. A deep sigh escaped Shane's lips, it was only a dream, a nightmare really. It wasn't real. He was safe. Strix was dead, and Trystan and Koda were here with him in their cave.

Shane sat up and wiped the sweat from his face with the sleeve of his shirt as Koda approached him. He pulled his pup onto his lap and began petting her soft ears and head, tracing her silver marking with his fingertip. Yesterday though, had been very real. He had almost lost his best friend.

Shane stood as Koda hopped down from his lap. He walked over towards his brother and gently shook him. Trystan continued snoring heavily. Shane shook him again, a little harder this time, but still his big brother slept soundly.

"Ok Koda, your turn to try," Shane took a step back and gestured towards Trystan. A smile crept along Koda's mouth as she ran and jumped onto the cot, with her small front feet standing right on Trystan's stomach, she began licking his face.

"Wake up! Wake up!" She said between licks. "It is morning and it is time to get up!!" She lay on his chest and continued to lick his chin and cheeks.

A groan came from Trystan's throat, and as he rolled to his side Koda jumped down. He yawned as he stretched his arms above his head, back arched, legs extended and toes pointed. Slowly opening his eyes everything was blurry. He realized as he rubbed his eyes, he didn't have his glasses on. Fumbling around below him with his right hand, he found them underneath his cot and put them on his face. Everything became clear as the lenses settled on his nose.

"I'm awake, I'm awake," his voice came out all scratchy.

Trystan slowly pulled himself into a sitting position and yawned again. Images of yesterday flooded his mind. He thought of their battle with the Booslaaks, what he had learned about his aunt and uncle, saving the Jibbetts from the Vargen, and fighting Strix surrounded by an army of creatures. Yesterday felt like an entire week shoved into one day. No wonder he was so exhausted. How he missed the comforts of his own bed and the breakfasts that Mom would make. As the thought of her filled his mind, he felt an aching pain in his heart. He missed her more than he ever thought possible. Looking up, he noticed Emiko had entered the cave and was staring at him.

"I see your worry and your longing for home," she spoke softly. "The time is approaching that you will be leaving us. What you have done for this land will be passed down through generations. The Tukki Tukki have truly returned. I have a feeling we will be seeing each other again. Until then."

She made her way from the cave and joined the remaining Guardians that had protected the cave through the night. As they were leaving, the Jibbetts were returning with handfuls of Sunberries and nuts. They bounded into the cave and set all they had gathered before Koda, deeply bowing over and over. She thanked them and looked up to her boys with a huge smile on her face.

"The Jibbetts, brought us something to eat!" she exclaimed.

Shane raised an eyebrow thinking to himself, *the Jibbetts brought us food? I hope it isn't poop.* After looking through it, he realized it was okay to eat.

They devoured the breakfast the Jibbetts had brought them in no time, and were washing it down with the remaining water from the canteens, when Shane spoke.

"So now what?" He looked to his older brother. He now trusted Trystan more than he ever had, and knew that he was their leader. This didn't bother him, he was chosen to be a warrior and that suited him just fine. Trystan reached over and grabbed his pack. Pulling out the prism's box, he was surprised to find that it wasn't pulsing with a light. In the past when there was new information for them, it would glow but it was still.

He removed the prism and it opened. He no longer needed to focus as he did previously; using the prism had become second nature to him. He scrolled through the *INDEX* and down through tasks. There was nothing. He looked through *MAPS,* not seeing any additional information there either. He was confused.

"Well," Trystan said, "I really have no idea. I guess we should pack up the cave and at least clean it up. We can fill the canteens at the sunbathing rock and try to figure things out from there."

"Sounds good to me!" Shane replied, excited to head back to the lagoon below the waterfall. He wouldn't mind a nice long swim after sweating so horribly through the night.

They circled around the cave and began closing the metallic stones. With the press of a button, their cots disappeared into their original form. Trystan began placing them in his pack, when he stopped and handed Shane half of them along with the flashlight.

"You should carry these Shane. I know you will take care of them."

Shane took the items from his brother and felt a surge of pride. It meant a lot to him that his brother trusted him. "Thanks Trystan!"

He put the metallic stones in his backpack and fastened it shut, placing the flashlight in the pocket on the side. Taking his Bo-staff he attached it to his pack and then put in on. He looked around the cave, it was like when they had arrived but it felt different now, almost like a second home. Trystan made sure he had his slingshot and canteen, and then placed the prism in his pack before tightening the leather laces. Placing it on his back, he too turned to look around this cave that had provided them with shelter.

"I guess it is time for us to go, are you two ready?" He turned to look at his brother and pup. The three of them walked side by side and started to make their way out of the cave, when the prism started glowing so brightly that it was shining through the fabric of Trystan's backpack and filling the entire cave with a bright blue light.

"What is happening Trystan?" Shane's voice was filled with wonder.

"I....I have no idea!" Trystan was puzzled.

All at once, near the large wooden trunk, the rock wall began to glow with the same blue light of the prism opening up a new secret passageway. They knew that this was the way that they needed to go. Turning around, they headed to the back of the cave, one by one they entered the small tunnel with Koda in the lead, Shane behind her with the flashlight, and Trystan bringing up the rear.

They had only been walking for a few minutes when a fresh gust of wind blew about their faces, smelling of tall grasses and flowers. Up ahead, they saw traces of sunlight breaking through the tunnel's darkness. They were reaching the stone chamber's end. As they exited the cave, they found themselves standing on a wide ledge on the face of a tall cliff.

Far below them grassy fields danced in the breeze that frolicked throughout. Beyond that there was a lake, the deepest blue and larger than any they had ever seen. They were so high up that they could see for miles, to the lands beyond the lake. They were dry and desolate with no greenery. There were large rocks and barren trees that made it seem lonely. It led their eyes to an area that was dark and thick. In the far distance they saw it, Trystan and Koda for the first time, but Shane recognized it immediately.

The very large, dark structure was a juxtaposition of black stone and crystalized rock. Haphazard looking and surrounded by heaviness, they could all feel it, even from this far away. It was as if it was sending them a warning.

"I saw that place from Strix's nest Trystan," Shane swallowed hard, "I had a nightmare about it last night. What do you think it is?"

Trystan was fixated on this evil place, "I have no idea, and I don't know if I want to."

Koda felt the fear that was coming from her boys and she didn't like it. She was thankful that in her moment of trying to figure out how to make them feel better, Arion slowly came walking around the corner of the ledge. The majestic creature had reappeared once again.

"Arion!" Koda barked, " It's you!" She wagged her little curly tail and headed towards the unicorn.

The boys shook the terrible vision from their minds as they turned to face the mighty beast and felt relief wash over them. He would know what to do.

"Trystan and Shane of the Tukki Tukki and little Koda of the Guardian tribe." His voice was warm and soothing. "You have reached the end of your time here, for now. This is not the end of your journey in our world, for there are many more adventures in store for you. You have learned many valuable lessons. It is important that you take them home, for they will help you there as well. You all have changed so much and learned so quickly. You have truly earned the right to the Tukki Tukki name and the magic you have acquired. But now it is time for you to return home. It is of great importance that you do not speak of your adventures here with anyone outside of the Tukki Tukki tribe. This knowledge is sacred. I need your word."

Trystan looked at his brother, both hearing the seriousness in Arion's voice, they nodded.

"We promise," they said together, and they meant it.

"But how will we know how to get back? When will that be?" Trystan's mind was racing with questions.

"You will know when it is time. Now it's time for us to say goodbye. I am proud of each of you. You have created an army of friends here that will be awaiting your return. In fact, I believe there are a few of them that want to say goodbye." The unicorn chuckled as he nodded to the three Jibbetts that were poking their heads out of the cave behind them.

The trio turned to see the Jibbetts that they had saved looking up at them with huge tear filled eyes, with their little paws clasped together in front of their chests. Trystan and Shane knelt down as Koda said, "Well come on then!"

The three Jibbetts ran to Koda and hugged her tightly, before running up to the boys. They scampered up to their shoulders, hugging them as well before climbing back down. Shane giggled as their furry tails tickled his neck and ears

The boys stood to face Arion. His silver horn began to glow intensely. Koda could feel its power flowing through her mark as well.

He raised his head and there before them, floating off the cliff's ledge was the door back into the Tukki Tukki house, back home.

Trystan looked to Arion and then to the portal. It was just floating there in space, hundreds of feet above the ground. His hands were sweaty and he felt a lump forming in his throat. He knew he had to be brave.

"Thank you for everything Arion, you are the best guide we could have ever hoped for, and thanks again for bringing Koda back to us. We owe you."

"You owe me nothing sweet child. You have the key to open the door. Now go, it is time." Arion took a step back as Trystan moved closer to the cliff's edge. Taking a deep breath and making sure that his backpack was on tight, he reached out with his hand, untied the leather lace from around his neck and slid the key off the end. Carefully reaching out over the ledge, he placed the key in the keyhole and turned it.

The door swung open and he could see the blanket hanging over the entrance. Taking a few steps back and rubbing his sweaty palms on his pants, he wanted to get more of a running start. Closing his eyes for a moment, all of the things he missed from home flashed through his mind. Opening his eyes, full of courage, he ran and took one giant leap through the portal and disappeared.

Koda, turned and nodded her head at her new friends, and then jumped bravely off the cliff and through the doorway. Shane turned around, raised his fist high in the air and with all his might shouted, "TUKKI TUKKI!!!" His cry echoed off the cliffs and through the lands below. The little Jibbetts returned his call and in their high pitched squeaks called back, "Tukki Tukki!"

Shane tightened his pack, making sure his Bo-staff was secure, ran and jumped confidently with full force through the blanket, leaving this amazing world behind him. He was filled with a new excitement and the thought of home.

CHAPTER 25

As Trystan came through the portal, he was surprised to find that he was back inside the fort. He lay there on his back, looking up at the blanket ceiling realizing they were right back where they had started. Where it all began. How had that happened? It had been three days in their Tukki Tukki life, and back at home, it was as if no time had passed.

Moments later Koda emerged landing paws first on his stomach. "Oooooff," Trystan exclaimed as Koda was now standing on top of him, looking down. Shane then came flying fast into the fort rolling through and knocking down all of the blankets and cushions as the three lay there in a jumbled mess. The room opened around them revealing they were home.

"Boys, I'm home!" They could hear their mom closing the front door, taking off her coat, her footsteps getting louder, the closer she came to them. The two stood up quickly, surprised as they realized they still had on their backpacks from Tukki Tukki.

"Shane quick, we have to hide them." They both took off their backpacks and Trystan was just about to run to his room to hide them, when Koda ran up and took the straps in her mouth, waiting for direction.

"In my closet Koda!" She almost seemed to nod to him as she dragged them down the hallway and into his room. He noticed that her silver marking was no longer in her fur as she left the room.

"Mom you're home!" Shane was so happy to see her face and gave her the biggest hug. With a confused look on her face, Mom looked down surprised by their enthusiasm. She felt Trystan's arms surround her as well. Koda joined in the welcome, jumping up on her legs. Even though the room was a complete mess, it felt good to have them so happy to see her. Hugging her boys so tight, she could not help but wonder what had happened while she was gone. Looking past them into the living room, she saw the mess of cushions, blankets, chairs, and pillows.

"You guys actually played?" Mom said smiling.

The boys stepped back just looking at her in wonderment and appreciating what a great mom she was, recognizing how much they had truly missed her. "Yes, something like that," Trystan said looking at Shane and giving him a wink.

"So did you guys eat dinner?"

"Yeah we ate." Shane replied looking over at Trystan with a curl of a smile emerging on his face.

"Why do I have the idea that you two have been up to something?" She didn't care. It was just good to see her boys happy. She had missed them. Trystan and Shane simultaneously shrugged their shoulders as Koda just sat up looking at her with a sparkle in her eyes.

"Okay, school tomorrow. You guys know the routine. Brush your teeth and get ready for bed. I am home later than usual, so it's really time for bed. But first pick up all of these pillows and blankets please."

Trystan and Shane did not hesitate or complain. They cleaned up the living room, carefully replacing each pillow and cushion back on the couch, and as a team folded all of the blankets. Moving the chairs back and looking around the room to make sure everything was in order, they finished quickly and both went to the bathroom to brush their teeth.

Mom stood there in the kitchen looking into the living room slightly confused. No fighting, they were actually working together very well. There had been no arguing about bedtime and not a single complaint about anything.

Trystan and Shane stood in the bathroom looking in the mirror as they brushed their teeth. Shane kept glancing at

Trystan waiting for him to say something. Had all of this really happened?

After brushing his teeth, Trystan turned to Shane and whispered, "After mom is in bed, come to my room okay?"

Shane quickly nodded his head. He finished up and put his toothbrush away. Both boys headed out of the bathroom and found Koda sitting just outside the door. Shane squatted down looking into her eyes and patted her head.

"Sleep with me tonight little guardian?" Koda looked up at him and almost seemed to smile. He stood and headed towards his bedroom. Pausing in the doorway he looked back towards his big brother that had also stopped at his door and raised his fist in the air.

"Tukki Tukki!" He whispered.

"Tukki Tukki!" Trystan whispered back, thrusting his fist in the air returning the gesture. He turned and walked into his room, closing the door.

Trystan looked into his closet, making sure that the packs were really there. Koda had stashed them in the very back corner. They were real and almost calling to him.

He changed into his pajamas and climbed into bed, his bed. Lying flat on his back, arms folded behind his head, he stared up at the ceiling. Listening closely, he heard all of the familiar sounds of his house. He could hear his mom putting away dishes and messing about the kitchen. He heard the noise of the TV in the background. The softness and comfort of his bed had never been so apparent to him, and he realized how much he loved his home. The smell, the noises, the comfort...yet... He could not help but drift back to all that had transpired. The adventure that they had was unbelievable.

It had happened though, obviously the backpacks were in the closet, but already it seemed so far away. His skin still tingled as he remembered the Booslaaks, the Vargen, and Strix. They had made it out alive. Were they going to go back, and when? He laughed aloud thinking of those silly Jibbetts and how they had entertained him and made him crazy all at the same time. He thought of Arion and the Guardians. How much he respected them. He realized that all of this had made him have respect for himself, for his younger brother, and their sweet pup that had come close to dying. It was at that moment that he felt overwhelmed by the entire experience. If they were to go back, could he learn to use the prism better to protect them? His mind would not slow down as he heard his mom's footsteps coming down the hallway.

The door opened and she stuck her head in. "Hey there Trystan, you okay?"

"Yeah Mom, I am. I am great actually."

Mom smiled at him and said, "Tomorrow is your birthday! I love you sweet boy. Goodnight, sleep tight..."

"Don't let the bedbugs bite," he finished her sentence. It was something that they had done for as long as he could remember. Then he added, "I love you too Mom."

He meant it now more than ever. He knew that he and Shane had a role to protect their family, and the secrets of Tukki Tukki. It was just something he knew. The prism was the key to everything. This was a truth he felt to his core.

Laying there for what seemed like hours, finally he heard his mother go to bed and the house grew silent. It wasn't long before his door slowly creaked open and Shane and Koda's two little heads appeared. Grabbing his phone and turning on its flashlight, he motioned for them to come in.

"Shut the door," he whispered as the two crept in and climbed up on the bed.

Trystan pet Koda while looking into her eyes. "I sure do miss you talking Koda bear." She placed her paw on his leg and gave him a deep stare as if saying the same thing back to him.

Trystan stood and went to the closet to retrieve the packs. Sitting on the bed, he handed Shane his phone with the flashlight. Shane never got to hold Trystan's phone, this was very different for him. He received it carefully, holding it and flashing the light on the packs. Trystan studied them each carefully before handing Shane his.

Shane wondered what had happened to his Bo-Staff, it had been attached when they had come through. When he looked closely, he noticed that there was a small keychain in the shape of his staff, fastened to a loop on the side of the pack. At first he was disappointed, but as he thought about it he knew that there was no way Mom would ever let him keep it. He was grateful that it had shrunk into a tiny version. He untied the leather ties and looked inside his pack. There it was, the large black feather that he had taken from Strix's nest. He ran his fingers up along its dark shape and sighed heavily. He remembered the battle and the terrible loss of some of their new friends. Koda sniffed at the feather and sneezed, it still carried some of the evil bird's scent and she didn't like it.

Trystan opened his pack and peered inside. The metallic stones were there at the bottom. Reaching in, he grabbed one and inspected it further. The button on the side was gone and it looked like a normal stone. All of them did. He stuck his hand back into the bag and felt it, the prism's box. It was the same size as it had been. Carefully, he removed it and set it on the bed. All three stared at the box, their eyes moving from it to one another's.   IT ALL WAS REAL.

Trystan slowly opened the box revealing the prism.   He placed it in his palm.   All of the magic appeared to be gone.   Try as he might, there was no opening it here in their world, but he knew that this prism was important and they had to protect it.

The two brother's looked up into each other's eyes wondering what could possibly be in store for them and what this all meant.   They did not know much, but what they did know for certain, was that their adventure was not over, this was only the beginning.

THE END

(For now...)

Acknowledgements

First and most importantly, we would like to thank our boys Jaxx and Shane for inspiring this great adventure. You have supported us the entire way and are the reason behind everything that we do. Jaxx, thank you for all your hard work with the logo design and website creation. We love you both beyond measure.

A huge thank you to James Harris who pushed us to write this series, you have always believed and supported all of our creative endeavors and for that we will always be grateful.

Kate Van den Brandt, thank you for all of your incredible ideas, images, and endless amount of knowledge in mythology. You have helped us create a story with deeper meaning.

Dee Stahly, thank you for reading this in its infancy and helping us piece together the frayed edges.

Cathy (Ketcha) Carder thank you for your hours upon hours of editing, for catching all of those commas and little punctuations that we could no longer see. You made our job so much easier and we could never thank you enough.

To our amazing parents, Sheila Rae and Charles Baxter and Jim and Sue Noga, thank you for everything. For the encouragement to be whoever we wanted to be, for loving us unconditionally, and giving us the gift of life.

Finally, to Raven C. McCracken, where do we even begin? Thank you for reading and re-reading this book almost as many times as we have. Thank you for your brilliant ideas and suggestions. It is because of you that we challenged ourselves to go further.

You are all greatly appreciated and we are so honored that you are a part of our tribe.

KRYAPRISMA

Tukki Tukki

Book 2

It has been six long months since Trystan, Shane, and their little pup Koda, returned from their first adventure. Their once vivid memories of that magical world have slowly started to fade and they have settled back into their normal routines of school, home, and family. When their Mom tells them that she is leaving for the weekend, the brothers begin to complain until she reveals who is coming to stay with them. With this news, memories of their adventure come flooding back and they can't wait to finally talk about it with another member of the Tukki Tukki Tribe.

Join us as Trystan, Shane, and Koda return for another EPIC adventure in the magical world of KYRAPRISMA